DON'T BE AFRAID

DON'T BE AFRAID

DANIELA SACERDOTI

BLACK & WHITE PUBLISHING

First published 2016
by Black & White Publishing Ltd
29 Ocean Drive, Edinburgh EH6 6JL

1 3 5 7 9 10 8 6 4 2 16 17 18 19

ISBN: 978 1 78530 001 1

A CIP catalogue record for this book is available from the British Library.

ALBA | CHRUTHACHAIL

Typeset by Iolaire Typesetting, Newtonmore
Printed and bound by Nørhaven, Denmark

To Francesca Meinardi, my sister

ACKNOWLEDGEMENTS

Many thanks from the bottom of my heart to my families, the Sacerdotis and the Walkers. Mamma, Beth, my lighthouses in every stormy sea – thank you. And Beth, thanks for the proof reading!

Thank you to everyone at Black & White, in particular to my editor Karyn Millar, to the goddess of foreign rights Janne Moller (that's her official title), and to Campbell Brown. Thank you Ariella Feiner, whose emails and calls from London leave me with a scent of oranges and a sense of sunshine all around me.

Many thanks to my friends, who put up with me and my writing obsession: Irene Parfimon, Joan Grassie, Roy Gill, Phil Miller, Simona Sanfilippo, Giancarlo Ferrari and Alison Green. In particular, many thanks to Phil Miller, wonderful poet, who wrote 'On Gullane Beach' for *Don't Be Afraid*. Phil: it's a privilege, thank you.

Thank you Sorley MacLean for the quote "but if I had the choice again", from the splendid poem "*An Roghainn*", "The Choice".

Thank you Scotland, my dear, dear Alba, and all the people I met and loved and laughed with these last fourteen years. You've been an adoptive mother to me – I feel like Ruth, who was welcomed into her husband's tribe. As the time comes for the family to go home – my birth home – to look after our elders, I turn back and promise I will never, never forget.

I always leave you last, Ross, Sorley and Luca: but only because you are the foundation of everything. A special thanks to Ross for the image of the long journey on foot and the deer keeping watch. I hope that one day you recognise your own talent for writing.

Daniela

On Gullane Beach

Raising a ghost with a brief touch of the sand,
there is a map, contours carved by a finger's print.
Or a frail guide for sound – score lines for unheard music,
rhythm, keys and notations. Holding that hand,
joins the pulse and beat of the waves on the land,
hears what you sung with your song, homesick
for the silence between waves and the soft tick of the clock
pacing blood, tides, the shot and return of our planet.
The pulse goes out and is returned, the echo in the seashell
a memory of light caught, rewritten and redrafted. We
are that ocean – presence and an absence in a small home of
                                              bone.
The distant waves float memory and deepen the well:
driven with mind, bounded by fingers, together and alone.
Your hand's song will be read; sung and forgotten by
                                    the beating sea.

Philip Miller

Memory

We were all flowers in bloom
There was softness in my body
And in my eyes
The promise of you

A woman stands in a field of swaying grass, a red handkerchief in her long, wavy hair and her skirt blowing in the breeze. The light of spring dances on her face. She is smiling, wrinkling up her nose, her eyes like half-moons as she squints in the sun. Not far from her, a little girl is trying to stay upright in the grass, which comes up to her chest. Her cheeks are red; her face is like an apple, fresh and pure and new. She is laughing and waving her dimpled hands like a little windmill, overwhelmed with joy at something so simple, so special: standing in a field of grass for the first time in her life. Suddenly, she loses her balance and falls sideways – the blades of grass have overtaken her now, they cover everything from view. She is frightened. Her face is about to crumple, tears are gathering in her eyes, her lips begin to form the only word she can say, the only word that matters for now, in her baby life – *Mummy* – but two white arms appear from nowhere and lift her upwards, towards the blue sky, then against a soft chest that smells just right, that smells like everything is good, everything is fine. "Isabel," the woman says, tasting her daughter's name, sweet as a song, "don't be afraid."

1

Candle

But if I had the choice again

Where I was, time did not exist. My heart did not beat and I did not breathe – so I couldn't even measure it in heartbeats and breaths.

It took me a while to fully comprehend that the fog around me would never go away, that I would always wander lost and alone in the mist. Sometimes I caught a glimpse of another lonely soul in my same predicament, sweeping close to me and yet so far. Solitude was my choice for refusing to go, solitude and despair. The absence of love.

And then, one moment in this multitude of moments that followed one another, each identical to the one before, I felt something shifting. At first it was like the tiniest whirlpool around me, in this windless place – and then a trembling all around, ripple after ripple in the mist. Suddenly, something began enveloping me and wrenching me backwards: it was pulling, pulling, like a rope tied around my waist. I was frightened, but the force dragging me began to feel more like a ribbon, a gentle, velvety ribbon that grew bigger and embraced me, a mantle of warmth, a mantle of love. I began to cry – Do dead souls cry?

And then, in the fog, a soft mother-of-pearl light appeared, and I saw the one who had been pulling me. She stood in a sea of little flames, some glowing feebly, some strong, some dancing to a mysterious wind, some still, all surrounded by light. Her words resounded in my mind – she was thinking inside my head. Her voice was so warm and full of love it made me cry: cold, dry tears that only I could feel and nobody could have seen. Another gust of soft wind came, and a faraway sound, a sound like slowly moving wings, invisible in the shimmering light and mist.

She told me everything, her voice a chorus of voices, some male, some female, in a perfect symphony.

They told me why I needed to return, and what I had to do. It was what I had been waiting for all along.

I couldn't find my voice – I couldn't even find my mouth to reply. Did I have a mouth? I looked down, searching for my hands – and there they were. I searched for my lips and I found them, and they felt cold. I looked down at my feet, and they were there too, bare and white. I smacked my lips together and prepared to speak, but nothing came out – I tried again, and in a croaky, feeble voice that hadn't been used in a long time, I said the word I'd kept in my heart all that time, all the time I'd spent in the misty, silent, lonely place: "Isabel."

Over the edge

Plucked out from peace
Second chance or condemnation
And the terrible, terrible knowledge
To bring with me as they force me off the brink
That the end
Could be sweet

Isabel

I blinked, my eyes sticky with sleep and tears, and in a few bleary, desperate moments, I realised I was still alive, unless heaven looked like my bedroom. Shadows danced in the corners – a soft noise of fabric flapping – the window was ajar. I had a vague memory of opening it last night, to drink in the view of the loch one last time, to take it all in before I did it. Before I fell.

My plan was perfect, or so I thought – Angus was away on a gig and Morag not due to check on me until the evening. When she brought in the groceries, she would see that I was asleep and let me be – I often slept during the day, because I struggled to sleep during the night.

Except this time I would not be sleeping.

And then Angus would try to get in touch with me once, twice, but even if he became alarmed by my lack of reply, I would still have time to do it before he sent someone to see if I was all right. Then, the morning after, Morag would stop by again with milk and eggs and bread, and she would notice that I was still sleeping, that I was exactly in the same position as the night before – and then she would *know*.

It was all set up so that it wouldn't be Angus who found me. It couldn't be. I couldn't allow my husband to see me like that, dead on the bed we shared – I could never, never do such a thing to him. Weird, isn't it? I was ready to put him through the torture of losing me, but I didn't want him to be the one to find me dead. Even in my despair I could still follow some strange logic that didn't make sense to anyone but me. It was hard to find lucidity in my thoughts. It would be hard to find lucidity in just about anything, if you had not left your house in a year and every day when you woke up you wondered why you weren't dead already, you wondered why the black hole in your heart hadn't swallowed you whole yet.

So I'd decided to give the black hole a helping hand.

But there I was. Alive. Though I wasn't supposed to be.

It had all gone terribly wrong.

I shivered deeper than I had ever done before, three times, as if my body could not believe that it was still working. I had time to register the horrific pain blooming in my stomach, the strange chemical smell seeping off my skin and the little orange dots in the crook of my body, underneath me – the pills I had taken too many of, but still not enough – when I realised that someone was there. I blinked again and again. There was a pair of feet on my carpet. Attached to legs. Attached to a woman I didn't know. *In my bedroom.*

Nobody comes into my bedroom, apart from Angus and

6

occasionally Morag. Nobody but us had crossed that threshold for a year.

My heart started pounding, and it was sore – like it was learning to beat again. Like the heartache I'd felt for so long had become physical.

I shut my eyes tight, as tight as I could, and tried to feign sleep – but the trembling of my hands must have given me away.

"Isabel," she said, and all of a sudden her voice came from somewhere closer to me – she was standing by my bed. I opened my eyes, but as soon as I tried to raise my gaze above the woman's legs, a wave of nausea hit me and everything spun. A stranger. A stranger in my room, beside me. What did she want from me? The million imaginary fears that plagued my mind cut me again – imaginary, yes, but real to me. She would kill me. She would make me sick with the invisible illnesses she carried on her skin. She would tell me I had to pull myself together. She would tell me that if I had any decency I'd leave Angus to live his life. And on and on, the catalogue of fears in my soul unfolded, like entries from my own personal Book of the Dead. Somebody whimpered – it was me, deep in my chemical haze, somewhere between sleep and waking.

I was alive; I was still to suffer.

Why?

Why?

Why me?

"Isabel," the stranger whispered for the second time. I wanted to tell her to get out and leave me alone, but I could not form words. I tried to shape my lips around the syllables, but they would not move. A kitten noise came out of my mouth instead, and something cold and wet rolled down my cheek. I could see, but I was immobile and mute – come to think of it, maybe I *was* dead, after all, and the woman was an angel come to take me to heaven. Except people who do what I had done don't end up in heaven, they go somewhere else: my father had always been clear on that, and on other things.

The woman kneeled beside my bed and her face came into view. I felt too ill to be afraid any more, to be anything any more. "Isabel," she said again – but this time, as she was so close, her voice did something to me.

Something I hadn't felt in a long time.

It *calmed* me.

My heart, instead of beating even faster until I couldn't breathe, slowed down.

I looked into her eyes, and I met a winter-green gaze. Her face was crowned by wavy brown hair and she smelled of cinnamon and sugar. How weird – she smelled of Christmas.

"Who are you?" I managed to say finally, and it came out like a croak. My throat was burning, and oh, all down my chest was agony, and my side. A horrible chemical slush coated my mouth and I longed for water.

"I came to see you. I came to help you."

I was ready to say *I don't want to see anyone*, but as I opened my mouth a searing pain shot through my side again. My whole body was sore, my soul was sore, my heart was withered up, and once again I prayed for all this to be over. I turned my head towards the wall and closed my eyes again. I was so tired.

And then I felt something touch me – the woman was caressing my hair, so softly, so tenderly that something overflowed inside me. I sobbed.

"Sleep now. I'll come and see you again," she said. As if her words had been a command, I felt myself drifting into sleep. For the first time in months my dreams weren't full of terror and grotesque images, haunting me. I dreamt I was standing outside, in the sunshine, looking over to a pack of wild horses across a swaying field – there were little lochs of shimmering waters and multicoloured clouds dotted all around. It was like I had jumped straight into my palette and all the watercolours and paints that lay abandoned in my studio.

It was a dream of hope.

3

Black flower

Take me home
Because the only way to be
Is to burrow inside you

Isabel

I can't remember much of what happened after. I had been falling, falling, when a stranger had come to see me and comforted me in a way nobody had been able to do in years, not even my Angus – and then I had fallen asleep. Except it was heavier than sleep, deeper – deadly.

Things happened after that – people touched me all over and shouted in my ears, calling my name, and then there was something on my mouth and I couldn't breathe, and the sky was purple, and there was the sound of a siren and all I could see was black . . . then nothing.

I was at peace for a while, floating in a medicated haze, drifting in and out of consciousness, all the anxiety gone. I had a vague feeling of cool, cool sheets under my back and my legs, and a cool, cool liquid being pumped into my veins. I wanted to stay there, but I was somehow aware that things hadn't worked out the way I had planned, that soon I would have to wake up. I wanted to cry but I couldn't.

I was swept away by emotion, a sense of relief because I

had survived, in spite of my carefully thought-out plan; then despair, because I didn't want to live any more; and guilt, wave after wave of guilt. But all these emotions were as far away as clouds in a bright-blue sky, as if someone else was going through all that, not me.

The sense of detachment didn't last long. Now my exhaustion was ebbing away and the meds were wearing off, and already my hands were beginning to shake. My heart jumped like a rearing horse as everything became sharper, harder. My stomach burnt and the corners of my mouth were cut and my throat felt bruised, and there was not a part of me that didn't hurt. Pain had come to remind me what I'd done.

All of a sudden, I realised that someone was beside me – Angus. I managed to turn my head enough to look at him, waves of nausea sweeping over me as I did so. My husband's face was white and his eyes were shadowed with blue. He looked crumpled, broken.

That was *me*, that was *my* fault – I was doing nothing but damage to the people I loved, I was causing nothing but trouble. Just like my father used to say.

And then, as I woke up another fraction, a million more sensations overwhelmed me. The room smelled wrong. The walls and the bed and the furniture and the air were dirty. The smiling nurse who'd come to check on me – thinking I was asleep and exchanging a few words with Angus about me as if I were a thing and not a person – was hostile. She pretended to be kind, but I knew she wanted to put me away forever.

Panic began to rise – I needed my home and I needed my window on the loch, I needed the kitchen table I sat at and I needed the way things were set up just how they should be, to keep me calm and keep this dangerous universe in check.

I needed to keep everything in the house the way it should be or who knows what might happen? The house could go up in smoke. It could crumble around me, or sink into the loch.

I knew it couldn't *really* sink into the loch, I wasn't delirious – I knew that all these horrific scenarios were creatures of my mind, but it *felt* like they could happen, and as I listed fear after fear in my mind I started crying and tossing and turning.

"Angus," I whispered – I would have screamed, had I been able to.

He held my hands, warm against my cold skin, and called my name. And then the nurse was back and more cool liquid filled my veins. Calm filled me once more almost immediately, and Angus sat down again beside me, still holding my hands. The nurse left again, with words that simply didn't register with me. I began to beg and plead with Angus, my words slurred because of the medication.

"Take me home."

"Bell, not yet."

"I must go home. You don't understand . . ."

"They say they need to keep you here for a little bit. You damaged your stomach . . . They want to keep an eye on you. There is nothing I can do."

"Take me home!" I pleaded again and again.

"Bell, I can't. Please," he said, locking his eyes on mine, his hand on my forehead. Oh how good it felt to have him near – and still, I had been willing to leave him forever. I was so torn between my distress and the instinct to keep living, my despair and my love for Angus, I couldn't make sense of my own feelings. Everything was confused.

I only knew I wanted to go home, back to my cottage on the

loch with its blue door and the rose bushes and all I knew, all that was familiar to me.

"I'm fine. I'm not sore," I said desperately. I needed to put on an act and pretend I wasn't hurting any more. I needed to lie. I needed Angus to lie for me and tell them I was all right, perfectly all right, so they would let me leave the hospital. A sudden blade in my stomach made me double over.

"What's wrong?" Angus leaned towards me. "I'll call the nurse."

"No. I'm okay."

"You are not. Let me call—"

"They won't let me go home! That's all is wrong with me! I want to go home! Here they're just going to hurt me!"

"Nobody is going to hurt you. They *saved your life*. They pumped your stomach," Angus said, and he let himself fall back onto the chair, a hand massaging his forehead. My eyes swelled with tears once again, but it wasn't because of my stomach hurting so badly, or the line in my hand nipping every time I moved. It was *guilt*, the guilt I felt when I saw Angus so upset, and that was a lot stronger than any physical pain. There was a moment of silence as the medicine in my system made me more and more dazed.

"What's going to happen now?"

"I don't know. I've never been in this situation before, have I?" he snapped. And then, softly. "Why did you do it, Bell?"

The question took my breath away. For a moment I lay suspended, breathless – and then my tears broke free.

"I don't know. I don't want to die. I just want to stop living like this."

"But you *can*! You *can* stop! We can go back to the way we used to be . . ."

13

The way we used to be. Before I got sick.

I used to be myself.

I used to be Isabel and draw and paint and laugh and make love and feel the wind in my hair and walk under the rain and I was Angus's wife and I was *alive*.

"I tried . . ."

"No, you didn't! You always refused any help. You refused your medicines—"

"I *tried* to take them. I really tried. But they're not good for me. They turn me into a zombie . . ." It was difficult to string words together when the sedative was pulling me down, down.

"It's *your mind* that tells you that, and remember what the doctor said? Your mind is playing tricks on you," he explained patiently, like a million times before. "And even if this crazy idea of yours was true, if the medicines were bad for you – which is rubbish – look at the alternative!"

I nodded, pretending to agree. I was so tired, so tired. I wanted to go home. I wanted to sleep. I wanted him to stop talking, but at the same time I wanted to listen to his voice forever, because it tethered me to *something*, it stopped me from sinking.

"The doctor explained," he continued, placing a warm hand on my forehead, slick with cold sweat. "It's just the side effects in the first few weeks that make you feel rubbish, then the medicines start to work and—"

"Please, Angus. Just take me home."

He sat back and took his face in his hands. He was exhausted, I could see it. I closed my eyes, so I wouldn't see any more. My Angus, what I was putting him through.

He gave a heavy sigh. "I'll speak to the doctor and see if I can take you home. But you need to promise me you'll take your medicines."

Silence.

He didn't understand. He didn't understand how those medicines made me feel. How many times I'd cried because I wanted to get better so badly, but I couldn't take those pills, I couldn't put myself through all those horrific side effects. When I first told the psychiatrist about them he changed the medication, and he promised me the shaking and the sweating and the anxiety would not be as bad, and they would last only a short time. But by then I was too terrified to take them again: they were poison.

I couldn't take them.

The doctors were wrong and Angus was wrong.

"Isabel. If you promise me you'll take your pills, I'll do my best to get you home," he repeated.

I had to get home. I wanted it enough to lie, not only to the doctors but to Angus too. I would have said anything.

"I promise," I said, with my eyes still closed.

"Fine. I'm going to see if I can find your consultant. A Dr Tilden, they told me."

After a few minutes Angus was back. He looked terribly upset, even more than before. He sat on my bed and I saw his face working, like he was trying to break something to me and he didn't know how.

"Look, Isabel . . ."

"They won't let me go home," I said, in quiet panic.

"I tried to convince Dr Tilden to let you go, but he said he needs to keep you in at least for a week, to keep an eye on you."

"What? One day. One day at the most," I said. "No more! I'm not staying any longer than that!"

"Listen. Bell, listen." Another deep breath. "He told me about your care plan, and it's going to be tough."

"What do you mean?"

"You're going to be assigned to a psychiatric team. They're going to come and see you every day, and phone you several times a day—"

"What? I can't have that! I don't want them in my house! I don't want strangers to phone me!"

"Bell, listen, try to understand. It's for your own good . . ."

I laughed a short, bitter laugh "No, it isn't."

"Why do you think they would do it then? Because they think it's fun? Because they hate you? Because they have some weird agenda? It's all in your head, Bell! These people want to help you. And so do I. Please, please, accept their help!"

In my confusion, I was convinced that there was only one way out of this: taking the lying up a notch. And if I insisted enough, if I were adamant about it, they would have to believe me.

"It was an accident. I was tired, and I didn't feel well, and I took too many pills by accident," I said, my voice cold and toneless.

"What?"

"I said it was an accident. This is all a big misunderstanding. I want to speak to the consultant myself."

"What?"

"You heard me."

"Isabel . . ."

"I need to go home and I need to be left alone, Angus."

"So you can try it again?"

"I never tried anything. It was an accident. I need you to stand by me in this."

16

"You want me to lie for you."

"It's not a lie."

"It *is* a lie! And if I do this you won't get the help you need!"

"I will. I will," I begged, suddenly vulnerable again. "We can decide together what I need to do. But please, Angus, having strangers coming up to the house and phoning me is not going to help, it's just going to upset me more."

Angus paused. I studied his face – maybe that had been the right thing to say. Maybe I had found an opening. He looked down and then rubbed his forehead once more in a gesture so despondent it squeezed my heart.

"Fine."

"It was an accident," I repeated.

"You are going to take your medication."

"I never meant to do anything stupid."

"You promise me—"

"I'll promise you anything, as long as you keep them away from me."

"Just remember, Bell."

"What?"

"If you kill yourself, you'll kill me too."

4

Lie to me

Say you still love me
Lie to me

Isabel

I had convinced Angus. We would lie together, and they'd have to believe us. They would have to send me home and leave me alone. Not completely – I couldn't hope for that – but at least I wouldn't have people coming to see me every day.

Dr Tilden was due to see me any minute now. I struggled to open my eyes through the sedative they'd given me. The pain in my stomach was now a dull ache. And finally, there was a knock at the door. A consultant – Dr Tilden, presumably – followed my husband into the room, and all of a sudden I felt a lot more awake. Would he agree to send me home? I blinked, trying to focus – the doctor was tall, and he seemed even taller because I was lying down, powerless. I sat up, Angus arranging the pillows behind my back. The doctor had a shirt and tie under his white coat. He and Angus spoke like I wasn't there, just like the nurse had. He mentioned therapy; yes, I had agoraphobia, which meant I couldn't get out of the house, but they could come to me.

And, of course, the medication. He could see what I'd been prescribed . . . and he listed the poisons I was supposed to take.

18

"Have you been taking them?"

A pause. I could see Angus was torn between his desire to take me home, to protect me, and the impulse to tell the truth. Because that would be protecting me, too. He settled for a compromise.

"Not as regularly as she should have."

That was my cue.

"I'm going to take them every day," I swore. Angus looked into my eyes. I realised I was not lying any more – I realised my promise was truthful. I'd try, I'd try as hard as I could. For Angus. For myself.

And then, it was time for my big act.

"It was an accident."

"I don't think this is what it looks like," Angus reiterated, reading once more the unspoken prayer in my gaze. "She didn't mean for this to happen."

Dr Tilden looked from Angus to me for a moment.

"I'd like to speak to Isabel alone, if I may?" he said.

"I would prefer it if my husband stayed," I demanded. I wasn't going to let this doctor decide how things would play out.

Dr Tilden and Angus exchanged a look, and the consultant nodded.

"All right. Isabel, I spoke to your husband about where we go from here. You were clearly greatly distressed yesterday, and I would have preferred to keep you here. However, your husband explained that he feels it would actually be detrimental to your well-being, so we decided you can go as soon as your stomach recovers – which will probably be a couple of days."

"It's true. I need to be in my own home. I want to go home tomorrow."

"Let's see how your stomach is and do a few tests. We can decide tomorrow, okay? But I can tell you already I think you should stay here at least one more day."

I was quiet. Two days was better than a week. I didn't think I could haggle for more.

"My condition, though, is that we follow you at home, like I explained to your husband. I have referred you to the Crisis team, and they will be visiting you—"

"But this has been a misunderstanding!"

"Isabel, I don't think I can believe that."

"I think it's true, Dr Tilden. I know my wife, and this was completely out of character . . ." I was surprised at how well, how smoothly he could lie. I didn't think he had it in him. *The things he'll do for me,* I thought, with yet another pang of guilt.

"I'm sorry I made everyone worry this way, but I didn't mean it. I had forgotten about how many pills I had taken, and my head was killing me. I had this terrible migraine; it was horrible. I fell asleep, and then when I woke up the pain wasn't gone so I took some more . . . and I hadn't eaten since yesterday because of the nausea."

"Isabel." I wished he would stop saying my name. Like he was trying to soothe a child, make her see reason. "The Crisis team is there to help. You don't need to worry—"

"I'm not worried, I just don't need it." He didn't believe me. Of course. He'd seen through my story.

"I think the level of support offered here is a bit too . . . intense. I think Isabel would benefit from a gentler approach," Angus said softly. Once again, the doctor looked from Angus to me.

"Isabel." Again, his voice was like nails down a blackboard. "I need to speak with the team, and we'll decide together.

20

However, I want to let you know that I'm certainly taking your point of view on board. We want you to feel comfortable with the care you'll be receiving from us."

"What does that mean?" I asked anxiously.

"That we'll look into a care package that is in harmony with your needs."

"And what would that be?" I insisted.

"As I said, I'm going to put this to the team. Laura, our social worker, will want to speak to you as well. But as far as I'm concerned, if you assure me that you really lost track of how many pills you were taking . . . and if you promise me you'll seek appropriate medical attention and appropriate medication for your migraine . . . we can maybe think of visiting you once a week for a month."

"I don't like having strangers in my home," I said, and immediately regretted it. It sounded like I needed help. "I mean, I'm very shy. I don't like talking to people I don't know."

"I see. Who is your GP?"

"Dr Robertson, in the Glen Avich Health Centre," Angus said. "She's known my family for a long time. We would feel more comfortable with her."

"I know her, yes. Well, I'll put it to the team. And I'll give Dr Robertson a call. Is that fair, do you think, Isabel?"

Patronising so and so, I thought, and I immediately felt bad. After all, he did want to help me. And his eyes were kind.

Still, I hated every minute. If only I hadn't called all that attention to myself, I could have been left alone.

"Yes. That's okay. So when can I go home?"

"Like I said, tomorrow, if your stomach behaves, or the day after. I'll let you know about the care package later today." He nodded briefly to both of us. "Take care. I'll see you both later," he added, and smiled a smile I had to admit was warm.

I'd made it. I was going home. But I had won a battle, not the war. I had to convince the social worker to let me be under Dr Robertson's care, then convince Dr Robertson I didn't need to be seen – that would be near impossible, so I might as well resign myself to a visit from her and be prescribed pills for imaginary migraines.

Most of all, I had to keep my promise to Angus – that I would take the medication. I couldn't let Angus down, I couldn't. My heart began to pound again as I pictured myself sitting at the kitchen table, those terrible white pills in front of me . . .

"So, it's sorted," he said weakly.

And now we were alone again, Angus and I. He sat on the edge of my bed, with his five o'clock shadow and his hair sticking up on one side. He looked immensely old and just like a little boy at the same time.

I love you, I thought, but somehow I couldn't say – I was too ashamed. It seemed like a contradiction – *I love you, but I'm putting you through this.*

No, I couldn't say it, not then.

At least if the tests went well, I had only one night to spend in hospital. It made me feel a bit calmer, that there would only be one sleepless night in here – watching the tops of the trees sway from the hospital window, gazing into the night, seeing it bleed into dawn. And then it would be morning and then they'd do the rounds and sign me off and then I could go home. If I closed my eyes I could picture my house, my bedroom . . .

Wait. There was *somebody* there, somebody who wasn't Angus or Morag. In my house, I mean. Or at least, there had been while I was lying semi-conscious in the unmade bed, among the orange pills. It was a vague memory, something I couldn't completely recall . . .

"Angus," I began, and then, as I assembled the thoughts, an image exploded in my mind. The memory came back, whole and disconcerting.

In my mind's eye, I saw the woman who'd come to visit me – I recalled her hand in my hair, the way her voice had slowed my heart. Her mossy eyes, her calm, calm smile – and then sleep, and the first peaceful dream I'd had in a long time. The ponds of shimmering water and the multicoloured clouds. The sense of contentment.

"There was someone with me," I said tentatively.

"Earlier on? A nurse, you mean?"

"No. I mean at the house. A woman *was inside the house, in our bedroom*. I don't know who she was."

"It must have been Morag. She found you." He rubbed his eyes with his hands once again – every gesture suggested his lack of sleep.

"No, it wasn't Morag. It was someone else."

"A paramedic, maybe . . . Or either you were dreaming."

I thought for a moment. Of course, I must have been dreaming, or hallucinating. And still, it had felt so real. "Angus?"

"Yes, my love," he leaned towards me and caressed my face in a way that broke my heart – how, how could I make him suffer this way?

"I won't try it again," I said. The words came out by themselves, from the bottom of my soul. In my husband's eyes I had seen a reason to live, a reason to be.

He placed a light kiss on my forehead. "Bell?"

"Yes?"

"How do I know you're telling the truth?" he asked, and his

face was so full of pain, I couldn't take it. He was desperate for a promise. And I *could*, yes, I could promise. Because I really, really, really wanted to try to live. Most of all, I didn't want to hurt him, ever again.

"Because I promise you," I said, and I meant it. Unexpectedly, unbelievably, I meant it. I'd gone from despair at being alive to relief for having being given another chance in the space of a few hours. Somewhere inside me there was a spark that refused to be extinguished. I wanted to go home. I wanted to be with Angus.

Still holding my hands, he locked his ice-blue eyes on mine. "I want to believe you, Bell, but I don't know if I do."

I took his hand and I placed it on my chest, right over my heart, right where the black flower was. "I'll try. I'll try so hard to recover," I said. I'd even try to take the medicines, every last one of them.

"I know. I believe in you," he replied. But that was another lie, like the ones he'd told the doctor to help me come home. Because in his eyes I didn't see belief – I saw fear.

5

Voices

Your words come
Like raindrops in a desert

To Isabel.C.Ramsay@gmail.com
From Emer88@iol.ie

Hey Bell! My brother was going through old pictures yesterday and he found the ones of that time we dressed as merry maidens and made him dress as a knight and we put on a play for my mum and dad! How old were we, twelve? You were Isabeau, I was Emerine and poor Cal was Lancelot! Remember? Remember we swore eternal loyalty to each other that day? You and me, not Cal, he was off to play with the neighbours as soon as we finished tormenting him! It was so much fun. God, how much I miss you. Why oh why did you have to go back to Scotland? Anyway, I still have those costumes, you know that? Look, I know you're not well, but please, drop me an email. You haven't written in ages and I'm worried. I'll go on tour with Spiorad soon, but we'll only do Ireland this time, for a couple of weeks. Next year, though, it's America. Things are picking up quite fast with Spiorad. They love the idea of a blind harpist! Roots Magazine *called me "the new Turlough O'Carolan". I'm just thankful I'm not called Turlough, now that would be bad. Maybe not worse than being blind. But worse than having red hair. By the way, have you noticed how the two people you LOVE THE MOST in the whole world are both red-headed AND musicians? That would be me and Angus. Me more, of course! Let me know if I can come and visit you.*

Please write,

Emer(ine)

PS. My mum saw your dad, Maura and Gillian in Eyre Square. I suppose you don't want to know, but my mum said that he didn't look very well.

To Isabel.C.Ramsay@gmail.com

From JSimpson@artistcom.com

Hi Isabel,

Just checking in with you – Marina from Usborne is a bit concerned she hasn't received your work for the Scottish Legends *book yet. We are late as it is. I might get you another extension, but you need to try to pick up the pace. I hope all is well with you. Give me a bell if I can help in any way.*

Joanna

6

Useless love

I feel you slipping from my hands
The more I cling to you,
The farther you fall

Angus

My love was useless, because it couldn't save her. It couldn't save Bell from herself. But never, never in a million years could I have imagined she would try . . .

I didn't even want to say it.

Maybe if I didn't put it in words, it never really happened.

I'd *tried* to be with Bell all the time, but to be beside her twenty-four hours a day as her own black hole engulfed me slowly was a special kind of torture there was no name for. If you sleep beside someone every night, and spend every day with them, you end up swallowing their joys and sorrows. And with Bell, it had nearly only been sorrow for the last three years or so.

My work helped me to deal with her illness, but there was a chance I might have to give it up, after what happened. I couldn't even think about that, anyway – all that mattered was Bell.

I'd stopped counting how many times my mother and my sister, Sheila, had asked me to leave her. Which was out of the question, of course. But that was how they saw it: like putting down a horse with a broken leg.

In the beginning, they were all sympathy. When Bell first started showing signs of depression they came to visit us, they bought her books and flowers. She was their charity case of the moment, and they'd help me fix her. And then things started getting really, really hard. Bell wouldn't let anyone in our bedroom – then she wouldn't let anyone in the house at all, which offended my mother to death. My mother just couldn't understand that Bell didn't mean to be offensive, that she was *ill*. That refusing to see people, refusing to invite people into our house had nothing to do with bad manners and everything to do with her distress. We lost nearly all our friends like that – only the most faithful ones remained. And that was fine, that's the way it is with people and mental illness.

No, wait a minute, that's not fine at all. That's *awful*.

Okay, what could we do? People are stupid. But my own mother and sister, they turned their backs on Bell, mistaking her pain for ignorance, not bothering to even try to look beyond. To their eyes, the pretty, sparky Isabel, fresh out of Glasgow School of Art and full of talent and potential, had turned into some Mrs Rochester figure, barricaded into our home. All of a sudden, she was an *embarrassment*. My wife, so dear to my heart, so beloved, had turned into a big problem for them. "Angus's wife has issues," they would say to their friends and to the rest of our family, hush-hushing the whole thing because they were inconvenienced, they were ashamed.

And still, my mother and Sheila used to love Isabel, in spite of what she'd done – what we'd both done – to Torcuil. They'd never showed much empathy with my brother, or consideration for him. They'd always openly favoured me, my sister following our mother's lead – which had always upset me, because I could see how much it hurt Torcuil. They'd barely noticed Torcuil's fiancée, but they certainly noticed Angus's wife. That was the way their perception worked.

Coming back to Bell – my mother and sister did love her . . . or maybe they simply accepted her. I don't know, because certainly if you love someone you don't throw them away when they're ill. Like an old, broken toy. So first they accepted her, then they tolerated her while she sank deeper and deeper into depression. But then they *resented* her, and they couldn't hide it. Actually, they didn't bother trying to hide it. If only their resentment had had its roots in their love for me, some sort of twisted, selfish-by-proxy protective instinct, maybe I could have tried to understand – but all they could think of was, I knew for sure, our family's status. And having a madwoman in the attic was not good for our family's reputation, my mother would have said if she had truly spoken her mind.

The only one who stuck by us was Torcuil, my brother. Even with the pain Bell and I inflicted on him years ago, when she left him for me, he still stood by me, loyal and steadfast. I don't know what I would have done without him.

Nothing, nothing could ever stop me from loving Bell, nothing could ever make me want to leave her. Not even what she had just done – *especially* what she had just done.

Not even if she'd tried to kill *me*, by killing herself.

There, I said it.

Because if she died, I would die too.

Let's not talk about that anyway. Let's talk about Bell, *my* Bell – the woman I married. She was a talented artist, her work was published all over the world and her books made many children happy. She had a studio in the attic, lying dormant and waiting for her to come back. Its door was closed, and I prayed and prayed that one day I would come back from a gig and I would see it open, and I would see Bell's fingers stained with paint again. And that expression on her face – that mix of concentration, bliss and exaltation, with a touch of absence, as if her body was there and her mind somewhere else – the expression she wore when she was drawing, lost in the process of creation.

I had an image of her burnt into my memory – well, I had many, but this one jumped out at me all the time, since she'd been ill – you know when you see something and it sticks in your mind, for some reason? One afternoon I came back from a work trip to London and she ran downstairs from her studio to say hello. She had paint on her face and in her hair, and her fingers were all the colours of the rainbow, and when she threw her arms around me she said, "Today I've been painting dragons."

That moment stuck in my mind. The way the sun shone in her long hair, the colour of ancient gold, the way she left smudges of paint on my hoodie, the way she smiled, the way her eyes looked full of joy, full of life.

Yes, that was my Bell.

And I prayed I would get her back, because life without her had no colour. Not even my music could give me anything more than a temporary respite; it couldn't save me from the absence of her.

Once I'd read an article about a whale whose song was on an entirely different frequency from every other whale's. Because of that, nobody could hear her. She sang and sang, but nobody picked up her voice except cold, soulless human instruments. And so the whale couldn't communicate with any other whale and she ended up isolated, incapable of sharing in a pod's life.

Bell was like that, I thought. She called out the reason for her distress in a frequency that only I could hear. If I stopped listening, she would be all alone. It would be as if nobody could hear me playing the fiddle – as if I played and played, but nobody could hear me at all, or they could only hear squeaks and strident sounds. It would be hell.

That was the way her life was, but I hoped not forever. I would help her find her voice again, in any way I could. I was afraid, but I had hope, even after what happened. Especially if she had no hope herself – I would be the keeper of her flame.

No, I would never leave her, certainly not if my mother asked, and not even if Bell herself asked me over and over again to go and let her be, to go and build a home and a family for myself. Because she said that: she said I deserved a family, that I shouldn't waste my time – her words – with someone like her. When she was really low, she said I deserved *a real wife*.

Well, I *had* a wife, and she was very real. I had a family.

I had a wife, a family and a home, our whitewashed cottage on the loch shore in my native village of Glen Avich. My wife was a beautiful, talented woman who, one day, went inside the woods and got lost, terribly lost, until she couldn't find the way back any more. But she would. She would find the way out. And we would all be there for her when she came back: me, and Torcuil, and Emer, and all the watercolours and pencils and unfinished illustrations that lay abandoned in her study.

One day she would find her way back to me, my Bell.

There was one thing, though, that I dreaded giving up, even for her: my music. Without it I'm pretty sure I would have lost my mind. The time I spent playing all over the country, all over the world, kept me sane and strong enough to go back to her. In fact, even before her illness, I lived and breathed music – it had always been like that for me. I was sure that if it weren't for my music, with the way things were, I'd follow her down the black hole she had fallen into.

I still remember the first time I picked up a violin myself, after hearing my grandfather and then my father playing for years. I think I must have been five years old, and the violin was too big for me to handle – my father crouched beside me and helped me hold it. After that, I never wanted to put the violin down, so I was given a child-sized one, and that was the beginning. Music was in my veins; I was genetically hardwired for it – I could never imagine doing anything else. But it was also a way to escape a fractious family life, my parents' unhappy marriage and my mother's domineering ways. I was sent to boarding school and then I went straight to Glasgow to study music. Torcuil stayed behind, too sick with asthma and allergies to go to boarding school, and then he was tied to home by my father's long illness. As much as I wanted to be near my father and Torcuil, playing my violin always came first – I suppose that was selfish, but I couldn't help it. I still couldn't help it. I'd made so many sacrifices for music, it had become second nature, as necessary as breathing.

Sometimes, to my shame, I thought that maybe even Bell had to come second sometimes, compared to the privileged place the violin had always had in my life, because when she was slowly sinking into depression, and I could see it happening, I was still away most of the time. I was in denial. Being away for work so much, for gigs and tours, had never been a problem before; we both pursued our passions, and she was perfectly happy to live as a musician's wife, with all that entailed. But when her illness began, she tried to keep me at home.

Bell was proud, and it was hard for her to show her vulnerability that way. And still, I didn't listen.

I wished I had.

And so we created our sick, bizarre routine, revolving around Bell's phobias. She didn't get out of the house, not even into the garden, so when I was away, Morag, our neighbour – a no-nonsense, practical woman who seemed pretty much unfazed by Bell's illness – would check on her and bring her groceries. I phoned Morag every evening to make sure everything was okay. Bell never called me; she was scared of the phone for some reason, but not of emails or texts, so that was how we communicated. It troubled me, to know that she wouldn't answer the phone if I called, but in a way, it helped to keep some distance from her when I was gigging. I knew that if I heard her voice, if she told me what was going through her mind, I wouldn't be able to concentrate, I would just drive straight back to her.

What she did changed everything, of course. Maybe, thinking about it, something was bound to happen, to disrupt the weird, unhealthy life that had been slowly suffocating us. Maybe the pressure had been building up all around us, waiting to erupt into something terrible, something life-changing.

The day before, the sky had fallen on me. Morag called my mobile and said that Bell was in hospital, that they wouldn't tell her exactly what happened because she wasn't a close relative, but that she could guess. She didn't spell it out to me, but I understood. I kept the phone to my ear for a long time without saying anything, with Morag saying my name over and over again to see if I was still there.

"I'm here," I said finally. "Tell her I'm on my way."

"They won't let me see her," Morag said, her voice shaken. It was so strange to hear the normally unflappable Morag sound so vulnerable.

"I'll come as soon as I can."

A few hours later I was at Bell's bedside. She was asleep, peaceful, no sign of illness or pain on her body – except for a line in her hand and the pallor of her face. She was so white, her hair loose on her pillow, so thick it made another pillow itself, one hand resting, open, on her chest. I noticed she wasn't wearing her wedding ring. There was a hospital bracelet around her wrist.

I sat beside her bed, mute, frozen with pain and disbelief. I had never thought it would come to this. I realised how naive I'd been – how stupid, even – to never imagine that she would want to take her own life. I knew she wasn't taking her medication; she'd kept saying that it made her feel ill and, stupidly, I'd let her get away with it instead of convincing her, pressuring her. I'd thought we would just plod on, survive the best we could, and one day this whole thing would go away as suddenly as it had started. But she did what she did.

So here we are, now.

On the edge of the black hole, ready to swallow us both.

7

Brothers

Let me wake you
Sleeping girl

Angus

A hand touched my shoulder lightly and I jumped – I'd been dozing in the chair. It was a nurse. She smelled of nicotine and something vinegary.

"Your brother is here," she said. Bell was sleeping soundly, her eyelids still, her arms by her sides, her chest falling and rising softly, so I slipped out to the waiting room, where Torcuil was waiting for me.

"How is she?" he asked, concern in his eyes behind his glasses. He looked shattered. I probably looked worse.

"Well, I suppose she's out of the woods. Physically, I mean."

"Come. I'll get you a coffee."

"I need a *pint* of coffee to keep going," I replied. After Morag phoned me I drove up from London through the night, clutching the steering wheel until my knuckles were white. I was exhausted from fear and lack of sleep. Everything around me seemed to blur at the edges and every time I moved my head quickly I felt slightly sick.

We sat in the hospital cafeteria, both dazed, terrified of what could have happened, what *nearly* happened, had Morag not found Bell in time.

It didn't bear thinking about.

"Is Izzy sleeping now?" Torcuil asked as he placed a mug in front of me. I noticed that he had slipped into using his old nickname for her, and I was too overwhelmed to feel even a twinge of jealousy, like I normally would.

Sometimes I wondered how much Torcuil and I had dealt with the past. Our history with Bell, I mean.

"Yes. Thanks for coming."

"That sounds very formal." He nearly smiled, but didn't quite manage. "It's the least I could do. How is she doing, did they tell you anything new?" I'd filled him in during an early morning call.

"Nothing new. Physically, she's in okay shape, apart from her stomach being a bit battered, the doctor said. But I have no idea what she's thinking . . ." I shrugged. "I don't know anything any more. She insists she's fine, but clearly, after what she did . . . Well, she isn't."

"Did she tell you anything? About her reasons . . . about what was going through her mind?"

"Not really. She said she won't do anything like that again. I'm really trying to believe her."

"God, how did we not see it coming?" Torcuil ran his hand through his hair, his nervous habit.

"I don't know. I blame myself . . ." And I *did*. Clearly I'd been too wrapped up in my work, or maybe I didn't want to see. Probably a combination. Or maybe, who knows, you just can't predict this sort of thing. Maybe some people carry a darkness inside them that not even the ones who love them can detect. And my wife was one of them.

"Honestly, Angus, I don't want to hear any of that. You can't blame yourself for this. I won't let you." He looked down. We were both stiff, unsure, embarrassed about this outpouring of emotion. Our family doesn't do *feelings* very well.

"Oh yes, I can blame myself," I snapped, and all of a sudden I realised how angry I was. At myself, at the world. At Bell. "She refused to take her medication, and I let her get away with it. She had this counsellor coming to the house, but she stopped that, and again I let her. She swore she was better, and I believed her. I *wanted* to believe her."

"We all believed her. She told us what we wanted to hear. And she is an adult; she makes her own decisions. You can't force her to do what she doesn't want to do."

"No, no, I should have convinced her. And now this happens. I should have put my foot down. But it's so hard, she is so ... *lost* ..." I struggled to find the right word. I felt my voice breaking and I rubbed my forehead with my hands. I really was at the end of my tether.

"Angus, listen. You didn't slip those pills down her throat. It's not your fault and it's not hers either. It's an illness, and you know that."

Torcuil's face was full of worry. He cared for both of us, even after what we'd done to him. Thankfully, he forgave us, but he was alone for years before he met Margherita. Some say I stole Bell from him, and maybe I did, but I'd tried to suffocate my feelings, and so had Isabel – we'd resolved not to act on them, to be apart – but we kept falling back together, like a planet and its moon. She was definitely the planet, with her vitality, her love of art, her beauty. Her *Isabelness*. I was her moon.

And so we had to break my brother's heart. We broke mine

too, because within my family he was the only one I felt truly close to. When Margherita came on the scene, though, it looked like all memories of past hurt had gone – finally my brother had found happiness again.

Happiness. It felt like a completely alien concept to me at that moment.

"I have to quit the orchestra."

Saying it aloud was like a blade in my side – but I had no choice. I was on trial with the Royal Scottish National Orchestra, hoping to gain my place soon. I'd wanted it all my life. I'd clung to my work while my family life was falling apart. Maybe I wasn't allowed to do that any more; maybe now I had to look reality in the face: a local teaching job. The occasional gig, not too far. Looking after Bell had to be my priority.

I'd worked so hard to get to where I was.

To give it all up felt like cutting off my right arm.

But to lose Isabel would be worse.

Torcuil took a sip of his scalding coffee and winced. "No chance. Isabel will kill you if you leave the orchestra now."

"I don't see how I can manage . . ." I began. There was an acid taste in my mouth. Like fear. Like sacrifice. "I'm travelling to and from Glasgow all the time. If they hire me, and I think they will, I'll share my time between Glen Avich, Glasgow and, let's face it, the rest of Britain. But how can I do this if my wife is so ill? How can I leave her?"

"Angus, you can't—"

"Well, do I have any choice?" I must have raised my voice, because an elderly couple sitting at a nearby table turned to look at me.

"There is always a choice. We'll find a way," Torcuil said, but I didn't believe him.

I loved Bell enough to quit, I was sure of that, but whether I could find it in myself not to ever be resentful, I didn't know.

I'd been faced with this choice before, when my father was ill: I was touring all over the place, and I barely saw him for months, towards the end. I couldn't make the same mistake again.

Torcuil knew what I was thinking. The words unspoken hung between us, my father's plea for me to keep playing, to keep going, while he lay sick. And Torcuil there, shouldering the burden for both of us, like he had so often.

We were at a crossroads, Bell and I, with this change looming in my life – both of us fragile, in different ways. I loved her more than anything. And still, my music . . .

It was never a case of everything revolving around me and my job – Bell had always been her own person, determined and passionate herself, in love with her art. I remember after we'd been going out for only a few months I was given the chance to go on tour with a band, and I asked her if she'd come with me. The summer was about to start, and I was already tasting warm nights and music and Bell and I together. But she refused. She was going to stay with Emer in Galway and work on her first illustration job for a children's publishing company.

"Are you sure? It would be amazing to have you with me," I said, a bit stung. Didn't she want to be beside me? I thought of how it would feel to have her waiting for me when I walked offstage. From the stage into her arms. It would have been perfect.

She smiled, and I remember noticing how the sun had already sprayed a few freckles on her nose, even if it was only May. "Not yet," she said, and held both my hands playfully.

"Why? What do you mean 'not yet'?"

"I mean, if we start out this way, you playing your music and me tagging along . . ."

"You wouldn't be tagging along!"

"I know, I know. What I mean is, this is your dream; drawing is mine. Would you stay with me and hang around while I work in Ireland?"

"Well, I couldn't—"

"See? I can't live somebody else's dream, and neither could you. But, I promise you, as soon as I get some time off I'll be coming to you wherever you are and we can be together."

And she did. While she was there we had three days of starry skies and balmy nights, and as soon as she left the heavens opened. Which was more or less what happened in my heart too – sunshine when she was around, grey clouds when she was gone.

She'd always been adamant she wouldn't be living *my* dream, but hers; now there wasn't much left to dream all around.

"We need to find someone to stay with her while you're away from Glen Avich," said Torcuil.

The "we" felt incredibly supportive and out of place at the same time. Like he had responsibility for Bell too. And still, I needed his help so badly. I needed all the help I could get.

"The doctor wanted to keep her here. I convinced him to let her go, that staying in hospital would harm Bell instead of helping her, so that was okay . . . but then he said she was going to be visited every day by psychiatric nurses."

"Oh, God. She'd hate that."

"Exactly. She freaked. I don't know how, but we managed to convince the doctor to release her into the care of Dr Robertson. Bell's satisfied, but I don't think it's enough."

"It's not."

"Do you think I made a mistake? Do you think I should have accepted—"

"No. With Izzy's state of mind, the last thing you want is to force her hand. But the fact remains, I suppose, that she needs to be looked after, right now. She really does. On her own terms."

"It's just that to phone an agency and find a nurse would make her bolt again. It has to be someone we know, and that will be hard enough anyway. You know the way she is . . ."

A moment, just a moment, of complete silence.

Yes, Torcuil knew the way she was.

He knew her very well.

But all that was in the past.

"Wouldn't Morag do it? It would be ideal. At least Isabel lets her into the house," said Torcuil.

"Morag works part-time, remember?" And then a thought hit me. "You don't think that Margherita . . ." Torcuil's girlfriend was warm, compassionate, cheerful – she would have been the perfect choice.

Torcuil took another sip. I'd given up on my brew. Hospital coffee was disgusting. "Not at the moment. Things are crazy with her work right now: her catering has really taken off and we have the National Trust visits at the weekends. And she has the children, of course. I don't think she could spread herself any thinner." Margherita had two children, Lara and Leo – a teenager and a four-year-old – who had moved with Torcuil too. Torcuil loved being a stepfather – he had come into his own.

Suddenly, I had an idea. "You know who I would ask?"

"Peggy," we said in unison. Torcuil had come to the same conclusion.

Peggy was the hub of the village of Glen Avich. She knew everything that went on, or nearly everything. From her little shop, a web of information departed and covered the whole village. The lovely thing with Peggy was that her gossip was never malicious – she was simply someone who loved people and their stories. If you were looking for something or someone in the Glen Avich area, Peggy was your woman.

"That's the plan, then. We'll see if Peggy knows someone who could stay with her while you're away, just keep an eye . . ." he said, and I finished for him.

"To keep an eye on her. To make sure she doesn't try to kill herself again." Oh, just thinking about it . . .

"Angus, don't . . ." my brother said, looking away.

"Well, that's what it is, isn't it? We might as well call things by their name." Just thinking what my life had become – what our life had become . . .

"Torcuil?"

He lifted his chin.

"Thank you," I said, and looked away. Meeting his eyes would probably have made me cry.

8

Two rivers meet

And every step we take
Is an end and a beginning

Angus

"Oh, it's the lairds!" Peggy said in a gently mocking tone as my brother and I walked in. Her small shop sold just about everything – food, toys, toiletries, stationery, even knitted outfits for babies. It was Glen Avich's little emporium, where the whole village went for goods and a chat. I wasn't often in the village, being away for work so much, but Peggy had known me and my family since we were children and she always greeted us warmly. I think she had a weakness for my brother – Torcuil's kind, shy manners made him a hit with old ladies. He was every granny's dream grandson.

"Hi Peggy. I was wondering if we could ask you a question . . ." I began.

"Let me put the kettle on," Peggy said cheerily, beckoning us to go through to the back. Torcuil and I exchanged a glance – she certainly didn't need to be asked twice. Right at that moment, the little bell above the door rang – a customer.

"Excuse me for a moment."

I busied myself looking at the community noticeboard while Peggy served the woman who had come in. I decided to turn my back to them and not look at the customer – rude, I knew, but I just couldn't bear small talk at that moment. Probably the whole village knew about Isabel having been taken to hospital – some must have seen the ambulance and some must have heard it from Morag, who, most likely, just said it in confidence to a couple of people, with the promise they wouldn't tell anyone. That was how Glen Avich worked. You couldn't even cough in your own garden without someone asking you at some point, "And how's your cough? Feeling better?"

From where I'd retreated, I could hear Peggy and the stranger talking.

"What can I get you?"

"Just the paper, thank you." She had a pleasant alto voice.

"Did you find somewhere to stay?"

"Not yet. I'm still at the Green Hat."

"Oh, that's quite nice, but surely not suitable for a long stay. I wish you could come and board with me, but my eldest daughter is home for the summer . . . She's here with her family and there's just no room."

"That's no problem, I'm sure I'll find somewhere."

"How long do you plan to stay anyway?"

"I don't know yet. Weeks, maybe months. Who knows?"

Torcuil chipped in. "I'm sorry to interrupt . . . but I know someone who rents rooms, Debora and Michael from La Piazza . . ."

"Yes, of course," Peggy said.

"La Piazza?" the stranger asked.

"The new coffee shop. Well, I say *new*, but it's been there for over two years now. They have a small cottage they rent to tourists. I'll give you their number, or you can just drop by. Have you seen it yet?"

44

"No. But what an exotic name! You need to tell me all about Glen Avich's tourist attractions." There was a smile in the woman's voice.

"Oh, we have an Italian coffee shop and a Chinese takeaway, and just a few months ago Ramsay Hall opened to the public," said Peggy. "And these are the owners, Angus and Torcuil Ramsay. This is Clara; she only arrived from Canada a few days ago."

"Nice to meet you," the woman said just as I raised my head.

"Hello," I replied, quite distractedly. But Torcuil greeted her too, and something in his voice made me look at him. He was studying her.

Positively *studying* her.

His expression was unreadable. A ripple of electricity ran over my skin.

I didn't have any of Torcuil's strange intuition – powers, some might say – but when my brother had that look in his eyes, I paid attention. My gaze moved to the woman – brown hair in an old-fashioned braid, a face that would make a sculptor happy, with her high cheekbones and striking features. Her eyes were a dark shade of green. Anyone who saw this woman would do a double-take, either because of her beauty or the timelessness of her attire – a long, folksy dress, a wooden necklace and long, dangling earrings.

"Why don't you drop by tomorrow?" Peggy continued. "Eilidh could cover here and we could go to La Piazza for coffee."

"Great idea. Around ten?"

"Perfect. Do you have a mobile? Somewhere I can reach you?" Peggy took out her own mobile phone from a nook behind the counter, holding it gingerly as if it could bite her and I smiled inwardly in spite of the circumstances. Torcuil and I exchanged a glance. "My niece, Eilidh, gave me this," she explained.

Clara rummaged in her bag until she found her phone. "I have one too, but I don't know my number and I don't know how to use it anyway!" She laughed soft and low and her eyes lit up. They were mossy green and seemed somehow familiar, though I'd never seen that woman before. She must have been just a little older than me – little lines around her eyes and the occasional grey strand in her hair gave her age away.

"Let me," my brother said, taking the phone gently from her hand. "Your number, Peggy?"

"Oh, there you are, here is my number, I have it saved under *Me*. See?" Peggy looked very proud of herself as Torcuil punched her number into Clara's phone.

"I'm going to phone you now, Peggy, so you can save Clara's number."

"Oh. Oh, sure. Wait. Do I have to answer?"

"No, just let it ring and her number will flash up, so you can save it."

"Oh dearie me, I've never done that before. Eilidh does that for me usually. I need to get my glasses . . ." She was all flustered now, and I had to suppress a smile.

"Don't worry, I'll do it. There. I saved it under *Peggy*," Torcuil said to Clara, returning the phone.

"It's ringing!" Peggy said, mildly panicked.

"It's okay! There. Done. Now you have Clara's number," my brother said with a straight face. And then, to Clara: "I also put Debora's number in there, so you can give them a call if you're interested in the room."

"Thanks Torcuil," said Peggy. "Oh dearie me, these things there is always something to learn!"

"Well, I'll see you tomorrow, Peggy. Thank you, Torcuil," Clara said, and the way my brother said goodbye to her made me look at his face. He followed her with his eyes as she left.

"What a lovely woman. Come, I'll make you a nice cup of tea and we can chat."

We followed Peggy into the tiny kitchen in the back. It was the first time I'd stepped through there, and I wondered how many stories those walls had heard. Peggy had this gift: people *talked* to her. They knew that she would keep their secrets; even if she loved a bit of good-hearted gossip, she wouldn't betray anyone's trust.

"So, how can I help you?" She put the kettle on and prepared two mugs for us – each had a little cartoon of the Loch Ness Monster painted on it.

Torcuil looked at me silently, as if to say *your call*. "It's about Isabel," I replied, squirming a little. In spite of trusting Peggy, it always felt somehow weird – even disloyal – to talk about my wife's illness.

Peggy, of course, knew that there was something wrong with Isabel. The whole village knew. It was just hard to talk about it. "Right."

"She ... she's really unwell. I mean, she tried to do something very stupid." I felt my voice breaking.

"I know."

I was slightly taken aback at that. People knew about *that* too? I must have underestimated the power of the Glen Avich grapevine. For a moment, I was speechless.

"She's coming home soon, but . . ."

Torcuil came to my rescue. "We can't leave her alone, of course."

I continued. "And I need to work. It's hard as it is, to make ends meet with my job."

"So you're looking for someone to be with her. A nurse, maybe?"

"No, that's exactly what I *don't* want. A nurse will freak her out. See, that's part of the problem, she hates doctors and nurses and hospitals."

"You might have to . . . I'm so sorry to say this, Angus . . . But you might have to find a way to convince her to be looked after . . . properly, I mean. By someone who knows what they're doing," Peggy said, as delicately as she could.

"She's followed by a consultant at the hospital, and we're going to speak to Dr Robertson, so we have that. But I want to try to see if she can get some help at home. Something like a . . . *companion*," I said, looking at Torcuil for help in explaining.

"Yes, an old-fashioned expression, but that's what were looking for," he continued. "A companion. Someone who makes sure she eats, takes her meds, and doesn't . . . doesn't . . ."

"Yes. I understand," Peggy said.

And doesn't harm herself, I finished in my mind, and my stomach clenched.

"She would have to sleep there too, when Angus is away for work."

"I see. And Margherita couldn't do it, of course; she is so busy with her work, with Ramsay Hall and her children . . . Eilidh has taken up some hours at Sorley's nursery and helps me here as well, so she couldn't either. Leave it with me. I'll have a good think, and—"

"Well, thank you, Peggy," I said, standing up. In spite of Peggy's kindness, all of a sudden those four walls were suffocating me. I needed some air. "If you hear of anyone, you know where to find me."

"Of course," she said and, to my surprise, rested a hand on my arm.

"Don't worry. We'll sort it all out," Torcuil said to me as we stood in front of Ramsay Hall. I considered how many times Torcuil had "sorted it all out" for our family, and what he'd got in return. Our father dying under his eyes. His brother marrying his fiancée. Our mother's patronising, unloving letters. And in the face of all that, Torcuil's unfailing loyalty and generosity.

"Yes."

My brother got smaller and smaller in the rear-view mirror as I drove to the hospital to see Isabel, wondering what I was going to find, hoping against hope that she would have shed the sadness and that I would find her smiling again. Hoping, as ever, for a miracle.

9

Dreamscape

We pass each other
In a dream

Torcuil

I was relieved to be out in the breezy afternoon. Meeting
Clara had left me slightly dazed. I was sure I had seen her
before, and I had felt something strange seeping off her mind
and into mine – an irresistible, painful thirst she'd had for an
eternity. Like she was looking for something. Like she was
searching.

It's difficult to put these gossamer sensations into words.

I refused a lift home from Angus. I needed to clear my head.
I headed up the High Street, not even stopping to say hello to
Margherita's mum and stepfather at La Piazza; I kept going,
past the little stony bridge over the River Avich, and all the
way towards the outskirts of the village. The chilly wind of late
autumn was on my face, blowing some of my agitation away.
I could not rest until we had found someone for Izzy, until we
had made sure she was safe.

I was frightened for her, but I was frightened for my brother
too. He had worked so hard to get where he was in his career
– and it was more than a career, it was his passion. Angus and
music, in my mind and in the mind of all those who knew him

well, were the same thing, woven into each other, impossible to pry apart. I just couldn't let him leave the trial at the orchestra.

I was supposed to turn left, towards Ramsay Hall, but, unexpectedly, my feet made me turn right, into the woods, and took me towards Angus's home – a cottage with a bright-blue door and a beautiful garden all around, standing alone at the edge of the woods and right on the loch. It looked like a fairy-tale house; and still, Izzy's home would not bring her happiness. Nothing brought her happiness any more.

I stood and gazed at the house for a little while, thinking about Izzy and Angus, a corner of my mind still whirling after the meeting with Clara – it was always difficult for me to calm down, to come back to myself, after having one of *those* moments.

I was about to step back into the woods – I would then take the long road back along the loch shore to Ramsay Hall – when I saw *her*.

I saw someone – a woman – at one of the windows of Angus's house.

I saw that her hair was very long, down on her shoulders.

I saw that her face was sad and tear-stained.

I saw her, and it was not a dream.

Her features were blurred, but for a moment I thought – could it be? – I thought it was Clara. But it wasn't possible. I must have been mistaken.

All of a sudden, I realised that warm tears were falling down my face, and I didn't even feel like I was crying, I was melting into tears of regret. It wasn't my regret – it was the woman's.

And then I blinked, and she was gone – there was nobody at the window, and nobody in the house.

I stood astounded for a moment, my heart pounding; then I

turned around, drying my tears, still reeling from that strange, alien outpour of emotion. I tripped over something – someone – standing right behind me.

"I'm so sorry!" she said, throwing her arms in front of her to stop me from falling. "I didn't mean to startle you . . ."

It was Clara.

I was speechless for a moment, wondering what she would make of my red eyes. "It's okay," I said, my heart in my throat. What was she doing out here in the woods, next to Angus's house? I was about to speak, when at that moment something started chiming and vibrating, and the noise broke the spell.

"So sorry, I have to get this. As you know, I'm trying to arrange a place to stay," Clara said, bringing the phone to her ear. I wasn't sure what to do – whether to walk away with a silent wave or wait for her to finish. I resolved to stay. I needed to know more about Clara. The way I thought I'd seen her at the window of Angus's house . . . This kind of thing happened to me sometimes, but not that often – when it did, I paid attention.

"Hi, I believe you were looking for me . . ." she said to whoever was on the phone. "Sure, I'll come straight away . . . Perfect. See you in ten minutes. Bye," she concluded, and took another whole minute to try to switch the thing off. Again I saw that she was of the same school of thought as Peggy when it came to phones – *Just press whatever, it's got to be one of them.*

"Sorry!" she said, still pressing buttons at random. "There! That was Debora from La Piazza. I'm going to see a room in her house."

"I can take you, if you like. My partner, Margherita, is Debora's daughter."

"Oh, what a lovely coincidence," she said, and she smiled,

laughter lines appearing around her eyes, lighting up her face.

"Well, you'll find everyone is either related or somehow connected in a village as small as this," I replied, and we started walking. On the tip of my tongue there was still a question: *What were you doing in the woods, so close to my brother's house?* But I could not ask; it just seemed rude, suspicious. And anyway, she clearly was out having a walk, it was as simple as that.

"It's Torcuil, isn't it?"

"Yes. Bit of an uncommon name. Scottish."

"It's lovely."

"Thank you. So, where do you come from?"

"Oh, down the road. Aberdeen," she said. "But I lived in Canada for a long time." Her tone was perfectly friendly – and still, something in the way she answered made me refrain from asking more personal questions. We chatted about the weather and about the beauty of the woods – but as we made small talk, the image of her crying at Izzy's window danced before my eyes.

We got to the bridge in a few minutes, and by then the walk had warmed us both up in spite of the cold breeze. I retraced my steps up the High Street in the opposite direction, and we arrived at Debora's house. I rang the bell and Debora answered with a smile, her black eyes full of vivacity, as ever.

"Oh, hi Torcuil! And . . . Clara? You know each other?"

"We met by chance at Peggy's," I said. "And then—"

"I was having a stroll in the woods and we bumped into each other," Clara explained.

See? She was simply out having a walk. Still, I couldn't wait to tell Margherita about what I had seen, about the mysterious woman at the window.

"Come in! I'll show you the cottage, then there is a *torta alle nocciole* waiting for you." Margherita and Debora were of Italian descent and both had a passion for cooking; there was always a small but amazingly tasty selection of cakes and biscuits on the go, both at La Piazza and Debora's home.

"I'm not sure what that is, but I'll certainly have some!" Clara smiled.

"It's hazelnut cake," Margherita replied as she came down the stairs. "One of our specialities. I thought I'd heard your voice," she said to me. Margherita and I had been together for over a year, and I still got the butterflies every time I saw her – pocket-sized like her mother, with a mane of black hair and the sunniest smile. I'd longed and waited for someone like her for years.

We kissed quickly, a soft peck on the lips.

"I'm Margherita," she said, offering Clara her hand. Clara shook it warmly.

"Clara."

"Come. We'll show you the cottage," Debora said, stepping past us down the corridor. We followed her out into their small, picturesque courtyard – right at the other side of it stood a small, stony cottage that looked like it had come straight off a chocolate box.

"It's so pretty!" Clara burst out. She seemed delighted.

"We hope you like it. The summer I spent here was very happy for me," Margherita said with a sideways glance at me, and I looked down with a secret smile.

"The first thing I did when I got your call was light the fire, so you'd see it at its best," Debora said, gently leading Clara inside by the arm. We let Clara and Debora step in, and Margherita slipped her hand in mine. I enveloped her in my arms.

"How are you?" she whispered.

"Good. Things to tell you."

"Any news of Isabel?"

"She's coming home tomorrow. I'll tell you all later."

We followed Debora and Clara into the cottage, and, looking at it with Clara's eyes, I could see why she was so taken with it. A sweet scent of peat filled the room, and the fairy lights on the mantlepiece gave a soft glow.

Clara walked slowly to the window – it looked straight onto the hills surrounding Glen Avich, covered in pine trees, a soft white mist at their feet. I stood and gazed at the view and the perfect landscape while Margherita and Debora showed Clara around.

"I love it! Thank you, Debora. It's perfect," Clara said.

"Do you want to think about it for a bit, maybe phone us later?"

"I don't need to think about it. If it's okay with you, I'd like to move in."

"Splendid! Let's go across to the house, have some cake and sort out the details."

"Why don't we go to La Piazza? We can show you the place and make you a cappuccino. I'll bring the cake along," Margherita suggested.

"You coming?" she asked me.

I nodded. I still wanted to know more about Clara – I was growing more and more curious.

La Piazza was unmissable – a big white sign in blue lettering crowned the entrance. A wonderful scent of coffee and baking enfolded us as we stepped in, enough to make your mouth water. The place had been a tailor's shop for years, austere and bare, but Debora and Michael had created a corner of peace and homeliness, with wooden floors and clean, restful white walls dotted with framed photographs. The glow of two fireplaces added atmosphere and warmth. We all sat on the sofas near the fireplace. Aisling, the waitress, appeared from the kitchen. "Hello there!" she called to us in her soft Irish lilt. As she stepped out from behind the counter with a tray laden with drinks and slices of cake, her enormous tummy was unmissable.

"Congratulations," Clara said kindly as Aisling approached our table, after having delivered the tray to a group of mums and their toddlers.

"Thank you."

"Aisling, this is Clara. She'll be boarding at our house," Margherita said. "Clara, this is Aisling. And her bump!"

"When are you due?" Clara asked.

"Next month. It can't go fast enough. In fact, I'm always so tired, I could just lie down and read my Kindle all day."

"She was due to go on maternity leave last week, weren't you, Aisling? But there has been a delay with the replacement. And she just won't stay at home, no matter how much we try to convince her!"

"I can't leave the two of you to do everything, can I? I'm waiting for my sister to fly in from Cork and take over the job," she explained with a pinch of exasperation. "She has this thing going with this Spanish boy, Pablo: one day it's on, the next it's off . . . It drives me up the wall! Anyway, she should be here any day now. Before I give birth here among the cakes."

"Now, that's a good way to come into the world," Clara replied, eyeing the glass-domed plates of homemade goodies.

"True! So, what can I get you?"

"A selection of cakes and ... cappuccino, Clara? Or a coffee?" Margherita said.

"Herbal tea for me, please. Mint, if you have it."

"Coming up," Aisling said cheerily.

Margherita got up and followed her. "I'll help you," she said.

"No need!"

"*Yes* need! You'll end up folded in two if you bend over those sofas. I know, I've been there."

"Will I send Michael to the Green Hat to help you with the luggage?" Debora asked Clara. "Michael is my husband," she explained. It was for him that Debora had moved up here from London, to set up a coffee shop near his home city of Aberdeen. Margherita had come to visit her, after having separated from her husband, and she never went back.

"I have no luggage. Only two plastic bags full of stuff I bought at Peggy's and the Welly. The Welly was Glen Avich's camping and outdoor shop, owned by Aisling's partner, Logan. I'm losing hope I'll ever see my things again! You see, they lost my luggage on the flight from Toronto."

"We need to go shopping, then," Margherita called from behind the counter.

"I don't know how much time I'll have for shopping. I need to look for a job."

"What kind of thing are you looking for?" Debora enquired.

"Well, I used to be a midwife in Canada, but I'm also a qualified nurse. I suppose I'll just apply to agencies, to start with."

She was a nurse. And she was looking for a job.

And I kept bumping into her.

57

I needed to know more.

"What made you come back to Scotland in the first place?" I enquired.

"Well, I have no family of my own, and I wanted a change . . . As I told you, I'm Scottish-born, so I thought, why not? I chose Glen Avich because a friend of mine was here on holiday and she loved it."

"That's why you don't have a Canadian accent," I said.

Clara smiled and said nothing. Margherita came back with a laden tray and placed a mint tea in front of her. "You couldn't have come to a better place."

"You are not from here either, are you?" Clara asked, tilting her head to one side. Tiny curls escaped her thick braid and crowned her head.

"How did you guess?" laughed Margherita – even though she had lived here for over a year, she still had a noticeable London accent. "I came from London for the summer, and I stayed. I loved the place, and also . . ." She smiled again, glancing at me.

"I love a romantic story," Clara said, and took a bite of her cake. "This is beautiful. So . . . *hazelnutty*!" There was a warmth about her, a sweetness that is seldom found. I was taken with her, as sometimes happens when you meet someone who seems to resound with you.

"So you'll be applying for nursing agencies?" Out of the corner of my eye, I saw Margherita looking at me. She had probably guessed where my mind was going. A thought, a possibility, was beginning to take shape.

"Yes. We'll see how it goes. I really want to stay here for a while."

"I'm sure it will all work out," Debora said.

The thought was getting stronger and stronger in my mind, but I would discuss it with Margherita before telling Angus or asking Clara herself.

Later on, Margherita and I were sitting in my study at Ramsay Hall. Ramsay Hall was such a big house, that we lived in only a few rooms – five, since Margherita and her children had moved in, compared to the three I used to occupy – and left the rest to the visitors for guided tours.

Lara was at school in Kinnear, and we had an hour before we had to go to collect Leo from nursery, so we had a short time for ourselves. She was nestled in my side, a stolen moment in the middle of our busy lives. But with all that was going on, we were crying out for a bit of time to think and take stock. I needed to offload all the worries I had about Izzy and Angus, and ask Margherita's advice.

"So you're looking for someone to be there when Angus is away?" she asked, and I felt her voice vibrating through my chest as we sat close together. Strands of her hair, silky and soft, were wrapped around my fingers.

"Yes. The problem is, we don't think Isabel will allow a nurse into the house. Angus struggled to convince the doctor not to send someone to check on her every day . . . She barely allows Morag in the house; you can imagine how she would react with a stranger. I mean, she even gets nervous when *I* go to visit them."

"Oh, I know. *I've* never met her . . ." she said. That was a thorn in my side – my brother's wife had never spoken to my girlfriend, except in writing, when Margherita made cookies or cakes for her and Isabel thanked her with a note. Angus often apologised about it, though it wasn't his fault – and it wasn't Isabel's fault either. Margherita didn't resent it, but it certainly saddened her. And no wonder.

"Yes. That is true," I replied, full of regret. "The thing is . . . Clara is looking for a job. She used to be a nurse, so she's qualified, but she doesn't have the trappings of a nurse as such: no uniform, no reports to fill, nothing official that is bound to make Izzy feel suffocated. And I have a really good feeling about her . . ."

"What *kind* of feeling?" Margherita asked. To anyone but me, it would have sounded like jealousy. But I knew what she meant.

"Well . . . it's difficult to explain . . ."

"Torcuil, you managed to convince me you see *ghosts*. What is harder to explain than that?"

Margherita was one of the few people who knew my secret, that I could see the dead. The Sight, as we called it, ran in my family, but neither Angus nor Sheila had inherited it. Instead, it had been passed down to my first cousin, Inary. The weird thing was that usually only women inherited the Sight – I was some strange genetic exception.

"Good point. Well . . ." I took a breath. "It's like I've met her before, somewhere. Like I know her already. And there's something else . . ."

Margherita raised her eyebrows in a silent question.

"I saw someone in Angus's house. A woman, at the window. Though, obviously, she wasn't really there. I just *saw* her there."

"What does it have to do with Clara?"

"Well . . . for a moment I thought it might be her. But no, that's not possible," I shrugged. "Her face was blurred, I can't be sure, and anyway it makes no sense."

"What was the woman doing?"

"She was crying."

"Right. I'm not sure if that's a good omen . . ."

"An omen? You're beginning to talk like a Ramsay!"

"Well, I *have* been living with you for a year . . ." She smiled, and curled up into me even more. I stroked her black hair, smooth under my touch.

"So, what do you think? Should I try to convince Angus to ask Clara? I mean, to ask her if she would help with Izzy."

"I think you should follow your instincts. She sounds perfect. She's here, she's a nurse, she's looking for a job. And she'll be living with my mum, so we can keep a close eye on proceedings."

"Mmmm. It would mean asking a perfect stranger to look after Isabel."

"She *is* a stranger, but Angus would get her CV, her references. You wouldn't go in blind. Also, everybody is a perfect stranger to Isabel. Including me."

"She doesn't mean it—"

"I know, I know. I don't mind, I promise. Well, I *do* mind, but I don't hold her responsible. What I mean is, you and Angus have a fight on your hands as it is, to get Isabel to accept someone in her home. If you have such a good feeling about Clara . . ."

"I do."

"Even if you saw her crying at the window?"

"It couldn't have been Clara. And we don't have that much time to make a decision . . . I don't know how understanding they'll be with Angus, if he keeps not turning up at rehearsals. He's only on trial, he's not a fully fledged member, and . . ."

"I can always cancel a couple of jobs, you don't need to worry about that. The problem is, will Isabel let *me* in?"

"Oh, God, it's all so difficult," I said, suddenly overwhelmed. Margherita placed a soothing hand on my cheek, her face upturned to meet my eyes.

"Follow your instinct," she repeated.

Yes. I would do that. I would speak to Angus about Clara.

10

The roads that lead to nowhere

It was always you and me
Against the world

Angus

My phone rang while I was in the shower, trying to wash away some of the tension from my aching muscles, and I jumped on it with a thumping heart. It could have been news from the hospital.

"It's me." Torcuil. I paused for a moment, letting my heart go back to normal. "Is this a good time to talk?" I was dripping on the floor, with a towel wrapped hastily around me, but I wanted to hear what Torcuil had to say – I heard urgency in his voice.

"Yes, of course."

"I might have found someone for Isabel. A former midwife and nurse, who's looking for a job."

"Right," I said, guarded.

"Remember the woman in Peggy's shop? Clara?"

"Yes. Yes, I do."

"That's her. She's boarding at Debora's now. Like I said, she's fully qualified. She's looking to stay in Glen Avich. And she *is* lovely . . ."

"But there's more to it than that, isn't there?"

"What do you mean?"

"You were practically staring at her in Peggy's shop. You had that weird look in your eyes. The one you get sometimes."

"You guessed. I had the feeling I'd met her before . . . No, that's not how it was . . ." A short silence. "I had the feeling I knew her *already*."

I said nothing.

"Also, I met her in the woods near your house."

"As you do . . ."

"She was out on a walk, and I . . . I don't know, I was on my way home, but I went to your house instead, and there she was . . ."

"So you met her again, and you had that weird feeling again?"

"Sort of."

"I see."

"But apart from that, she is *qualified* . . ."

"You said that already."

"I think she's worth talking to."

A pause, while I took a moment to think. I didn't want to be on the phone too long in case the hospital called.

"I have her number . . ." he said again, sheepishly.

"Fine. You convinced me. I'll call Clara, and see what's what."

11

The way I simply love you

When I call and say
Everything is just too much
When I call and say
Please watch over me

Angus

"Clara? It's Angus Ramsay here. I'm sorry to bother you."

"Oh, hello," she said in an even, tranquil voice. As if she was not surprised at all.

"My brother gave me your number . . . I was wondering if we could have a chat. About a job."

"Yes."

"A sort of nursing job. Home care, I think you'd call it."

"Sure. That sounds right up my street."

Again, that calm, that poise. But why wasn't she asking more questions? Maybe she wanted to do it in person.

"Can we meet up today?" I ventured. Bell was coming home from the hospital the next day, so I wanted to sort everything out before then. That was more than I dared hope for.

"Certainly. Where?"

"Ramsay Hall? Around four?" I hadn't asked them yet, but I was sure that Torcuil and Margherita would be fine with it. It just didn't feel right to take people to the house while Bell wasn't here – it would have been like a violation, in a way.

"Perfect. I'll ask Debora for directions. See you later, then. I'll bring my paperwork, so you can see my qualifications and references."

"Great. Thank you, I know it's short notice . . ."

"That's not a problem."

Still not curious about what the job was? If it were me, I would have liked to have at least a general idea. But she still wasn't asking any questions, so I took it upon myself to explain more. Just in case she decided then that it wasn't for her.

"It's about my wife, Isabel. She suffers from . . . well, the doctors say she's depressed"

"I understand."

Did she? Did she really understand the extent of it? Of course not. She might not even have known Bell was in hospital, and the reason for it – unless she'd picked it up on the Glen Avich grapevine. Oh, it was hard to explain. And what if Clara felt it was all too much?

But Torcuil had said he had a *good feeling* about her.

And Torcuil knew things in strange ways.

"So, see you later," I said, and I realised my heart was in my throat. It was difficult to talk about Bell, even in a roundabout way. And so much rested on this. So much rested on making sure Bell was safe.

"I'll be there. Thank you."

"No, thank *you*," I said, and I meant it.

"Oh, and Angus?"

"Yes?"

"Is Isabel in agreement? I mean, about someone looking after her?"

66

Good question. That was what was worrying me. One of the million things worrying me, really.

I chose my words carefully. "She is and she isn't. I mean . . . she doesn't know about you. But I think she is ready to try to sort things out. For her, for me. For our family." My voice was beginning to shake. I needed to stop talking.

That was the thing. I hadn't discussed this with Bell yet.

And it was quite a problem, because I knew for sure she was going to resist with all her might.

12

Weaving

If only I could
Unearth the seeds of destruction
For you I would grow
Sunflowers

Angus

I walked along the loch shore, the grass still wet and shiny with
dew, white mist rising from the fields – like a dreamscape.
The water lapped the shore softly and broke the silence with
infinite sweetness – there was never an endless, barren silence
around the loch, but a silence that was brimming with life.
Its calm seeped inside me, in spite of the chaos in my life.
That moment was worlds away from the upset and grief of
my home life. And still, one thought kept whirling in the back
of my mind – would I be able to keep Bell safe? Safe from her
illness, safe from herself? I was waiting for the time she would
come home with a mixture of longing and apprehension. Our
bed was so empty without her; the house was so empty. I just
wanted her back.

I could smell winter on the wind that day. I could see it in the
water shining green, rippling softly in the breeze. Autumn was
over and the cold days were on their way. My gaze rested on
Ailsa, the little island in the middle of the loch. It was covered

in larches and pine trees, bent by years and years of wind, and it rose from the water like a mystical vision. When my heart was lighter and my mind clearer, I would come here with my violin and turn the beauty all around me into yet another tune, to add to the many I'd written for this place already.

I came to a stone arch with an iron gate at its centre, just ajar, ready for me. Ramsay Hall sat at the centre of a gravelled space – this was where I grew up, and the ancestral home of my family. It was slowly falling into disrepair, too big for us to look after, and there was no money in the family pot – but Torcuil and Margherita had turned all that around. I couldn't help looking around me in awe of what they'd done. The first thing I saw was the wooden hut, then closed, where tickets were sold, and a National Trust sign just beside it, with a map and opening hours. And then the house, as beautiful as ever, carved in grey sandstone, with a square central building and two wings at its sides. Mighty oak trees, hundreds of years old, surrounded the house like a crown, and deer roamed in fields of grass. From the outbuildings came the low, gentle neighing of a horse.

I walked along the back wall until I reached a small wooden door painted black. It was garlanded by a stunning fuchsia plant, still laden with flowers before winter stripped it with its freezing temperatures. Lined up against the wall were pots of heather – Margherita's touch. In spring and summer, Margherita's pots overflowed with brightly coloured flowers. I remembered how unkempt the gardens looked before she came along. In a way, they looked like Torcuil felt – lonely. But not any more.

"Angus," my brother greeted me as I knocked softly and let myself in. He still had blue shadows under his eyes. The last few days had taken a lot out of both of us.

"Cup of tea? I made some *torta di mele* . . . apple cake," said Margherita with a smile. She always had a reason to smile. I didn't think I'd ever seen her grumpy in all the time I'd known her – since that evening when she came to hear me playing and I guessed Torcuil's feelings for her with just one look.

"Thanks. Sorry, I'm a bit early," I said, taking a seat at their kitchen table, full of Torcuil's papers and books. He must have been working.

"No problem. Clara is due here in ten—"

"Hello?" A pleasant alto voice, coming from outside, interrupted me.

"Hello, come on in!" Margherita got up to open the kitchen door and welcome Clara. She stepped in with a smile that made her eyes crinkle up, her brown hair piled softly on top of her head in an old-fashioned hairdo. I had thought she probably was around my and Torcuil's age, mid-thirties, but that day she seemed ageless. Very old or very young, depending on how you looked at her.

"Sorry, I'm early," she said, echoing my words.

"Don't worry, we were all ready. Can I get you some mint tea and apple cake?" Margherita offered.

"Oh, you remembered I like mint tea! Thank you, Margherita."

"Take a seat," Torcuil said. "Sorry, I'll move some of my stuff . . ."

"He can't help it," Margherita laughed. "He is naturally messy!"

"All these books . . . What do you do, Torcuil?" asked Clara.

"I'm a lecturer. I teach history in Edinburgh. And Angus is a musician."

"What do you play?"

70

"I play the fiddle . . . but tell us about your job. So you were a nurse for years, both in Canada and here?"

"A midwife, actually. Here, I have all the paperwork . . . Thankfully I kept all the important stuff in my hand luggage! The rest of my things are probably in Brazil or something. They lost my luggage," she explained, handing me a blue folder. We went through her certificates and references while Margherita placed a steaming cup of mint tea in front of her.

"What exactly are you looking for?" Clara asked, wrapping her fingers around the warm cup. I had to say what was in all our minds: *Someone who will watch my wife so she doesn't try anything stupid again.*

"Someone to keep Isabel company when I'm not around, which, sadly, is often. Someone to see she takes her medicines, who distracts her a little . . ."

Clara was calm. "I find it difficult to accept you would trust me with your wife when you know me so little," she said, her moss-green eyes clear, open.

Torcuil pushed his glasses up his nose. "Call it skin-deep. We have the feeling you might be the right person."

"And anyway, the first obstacle is to see if Isabel will let you in the house at all," I intervened.

"And would you need me to stay over, sometimes? I mean, if you're a musician . . . Are you away overnight often?"

I opened my arms. "Look, it's my job. It's my life. I know I should always be there, but—"

"No, you shouldn't." Torcuil looked at me, raising his eyebrows. "You do what you do. If you were to give it up for Isabel . . . You would never forgive her. And she would never forgive herself."

I looked down. I was so lucky to have my brother, always in my corner. Weird, though: we were talking about these family matters in front of Clara and it didn't seem wrong.

"Anyway," I continued. "This is an especially difficult time for my work. I'm on trial with the Scottish National Orchestra. There are two possibilities here: I stop the trial—"

"Or *I* work out." Clara finished the sentence for me.

"No pressure, then." Torcuil attempted a joke.

"It's a lot to take on," I said.

"But she is the one for us," my brother intervened, again looking at me. My arms came out in goose bumps. *What does he know?* Like so often with Torcuil, the workings of his mind were a mystery. I could only trust. And I did. I *did* trust him.

"I think I am," Clara said with a smile. She was still calm, unfazed.

"I haven't told you everything. Bell . . . Isabel is not here at the moment. She's at the hospital. She . . ." I couldn't say it aloud. I couldn't.

She tried to kill herself.

For a moment, there was silence around the table, and I could almost feel Torcuil and Margherita holding their breath.

"I know," Clara said in a soft voice.

"I suppose there is no point in asking you *how* you know." I was trying to keep my voice steady, but I couldn't help my distress creeping in. I cleared my throat.

"It's a small village . . ."

"So you are aware of what we are dealing with?"

"Yes."

I took a breath. "If you want it, the job is yours. What do you say?"

"I say, yes. If Isabel wants me . . ."

"We'll persuade her," said Torcuil, but he was tormenting a tea towel in a way that told me he was not *that* confident.

I looked around at everyone. "Well, that's the easy part done." I felt a lump in my throat. *Please let me persuade her*, I prayed silently. *Please convince Bell to let Clara into her life.* But I knew it didn't work like that – ultimately, Bell would make her own decision. It would be up to her to accept Clara or not.

To try to walk on the road to recovery, or stand still and suffer.

All the help in the world was there, if she accepted it.

My Bell. My Bell and her battle.

"You wouldn't give me a guided tour of this beautiful place?" Clara asked, and with that, the tension burst like a bubble.

We walked through room after room, each of them spotless, with the most beautiful furniture pieces. Dotted here and there were signs from the National Trust, explaining the history and use of each room. It was strange, to see these spaces we used to live in as children cordoned off and shown to the public. I remembered playing hide-and-seek here with my siblings, reading books on the antique sofas, stepping without thinking on the precious mosaicked floor of the music room, keeping our clothes in the intricately carved wardrobes, sitting for dinner in the light of precious chandeliers. It was all normal, for us. Just the way life was.

"Look, there's even a treasure hunt you can do. For children," Torcuil said, handing Clara a piece of paper. "Margherita's son – he's four now – must have done it a hundred times!"

"Let me see. Find the beast of the north . . . Oh, up there!" She pointed to the big framed painting of a polar bear. "My children would have loved this too, when they were little."

"You have children?" asked Margherita. But Clara was not forthcoming.

"This is great. You are so fortunate to live in such a beautiful place . . ." she said, gesturing to encompass it all.

"It was Margherita. She turned this place around." Torcuil gazed at Margherita for a moment, and the love was evident in his eyes. I was reminded of what had been between Isabel and Torcuil, and how it was now truly buried.

"Not true! You did just as much!" Margherita protested, but he shook his head.

Finally, Torcuil opened a set of double wooden doors and led us into the grand hall, its ceiling painted blue and dotted with silver stars and baby angels. Clara couldn't take her eyes off the fresco, and she wandered around for a while, looking up.

"And that, there, is my house." I pointed to one of the enormous arched windows. Among the greenery, we could see the whitewashed cottage standing alone across the loch.

I imagined Bell there, waiting for me.

We stood outside in the chilly afternoon air. Now that the decision had been made, I was a bit calmer. Clara's serenity seemed to have rubbed off on me, at least to some degree.

"So, tomorrow at ten? I'll text you if there are any problems . . . I mean, if Bell really is adamant that she's not ready to see you we can work around it, and rearrange . . ."

"Tomorrow," Torcuil repeated, and our eyes met. I could feel we shared the same trepidation, but we also shared the same hope. "She will let Clara in. I *know* it."

I wasn't so sure, but I knew I would do anything in my power to make this happen.

"We'll be fine," Clara said, and again I felt like I could breathe.

Margherita broke the short silence. "I was wondering . . . I need to go and get my son at my mum's, but why don't you stay for dinner?"

"You're very kind, but tonight I'd rather be on my own. There is so much to take in, and I'm still a bit jet-lagged."

Margherita was sympathetic. "You must be. It's a long way from Canada."

"A long way indeed," said Torcuil, and once again he looked at Clara in a way I couldn't decipher.

I, too, turned down the invitation to stay at Ramsay Hall. I needed time to think. I spent the evening alone, sitting at the window, listening to music. I watched day turn to night and wished it was time to see Bell already, to have her back here, where she belonged.

And then, after a few hours of tormented sleep and two cups of strong coffee, it was time to go to the hospital and finally, finally take Bell home.

13

Prison

The place I love the most
Becomes my prison
The world is just a space
Inside my weary heart

Isabel

When I came back from hospital, everything was exactly how I left it. I couldn't have handled it if Morag had come and touched my things, and Angus knew that. Only the bed was made, the little orange dots of my nightmare gone. Looking at the bed made me feel sick.

I'd spent the journey home obsessively listening to *The Singing Wheel,* my friend Emer's CD, and trying to forget I was actually *outside.* As we went through the garden, Angus tried to show me how lovely our late-blooming roses still were – but I preferred the view of my garden from the inside. I stepped into the kitchen, my husband following me with the little bag of my belongings, and then up the stairs, slowly.

I was so happy to be home.

I was devastated to be back in my prison.

I was neither. I was hollow. I was nothing.

I stopped for a moment in front of the mirror hanging on the landing and studied the shape of my head. I often wondered what had gone wrong in there. Was it an illness? Was it a choice, a personality trait? Was this happening because of what I went through when I was a child?

Maybe it didn't even matter.

"Bell?" Angus beckoned me up the stairs.

"Yes. Coming."

I went through the motions. Angus was there with me, murmuring words of encouragement and looking after me, sweet as a mother. I had a long, hot shower to wash the hospital smell off my skin, the water flowing over me like a cleansing waterfall. I noticed that there was a new set of soaps there, white with cinnamon sticks and mint leaves and bits of orange skins worked into them – I recognised Anne's handiwork, my old school friend. She must have sent them while I was at the hospital. It seemed to me that Glen Avich had found a way to show it had not forgotten me, even in my self-imposed exile. Tears started prickling behind my eyes, and then fell silently, now that Angus couldn't see me. Weird how when you've come so close to death, something like the scent of homemade soap is such a blessing. *I'm still alive to feel this,* my body whispered.

I sat at the window seat in my bedroom and I switched on my laptop. I was scared of phones, but I was okay with computers. Weird, I know.

Dozens of emails from Emer, panicking because of my silence. Oh God, I really hurt everyone who loves me, don't I?

I switched it off without replying. What was I supposed to say? *Hi Emer, so lovely to hear from you, I tried to kill myself?*

I looked outside, resting my head on the windowpane. It felt cool against my cheek. The view was so familiar I could have drawn it with my eyes closed. Angus had plugged my hairdryer in and laid out the brush that had been my mother's.

He was as thoughtful, as loving as ever – but he would not meet my eyes. Every time our gazes linked, he looked away, he busied himself with something else.

Maybe he couldn't look my despair in the eye, it was too painful for him, or maybe he was angry and he couldn't show me, he didn't want me to see.

I didn't blame him for being angry. I had everything: I had his love, friends, a beautiful home and a job I adored. But I had fallen anyway.

I had fallen into the black hole.

Could I climb out? Would I be able to do that? I had to. I couldn't leave Angus broken the way I was.

But the other day, when downing the orange pills had seemed the only option left, thinking of Angus hadn't been enough. Just the opposite: it seemed to me that he would have been better off without me, that I was doing him a favour. It really felt that way.

"Bell, listen, I'll just give Torcuil a phone and see if he can get some stuff in for us. I completely forgot to buy food and Morag doesn't seem to have left anything edible . . ."

I managed a little smile. Morag's taste in food was an inside joke between us: she bought blocks of fatty cheap cheese and anaemic sausages, long-life milk, chemical sliced bread, a bottle of ketchup. And tinned peaches, for vitamins.

"What did she get?"

"Campbell's mushroom soup and a can of haggis."

"Nice."

"Yes. So I'll just give him a phone, and if it's okay with you to see him . . ."

"It's okay. You go and get food. I'll be fine, I promise. I mean, I'd love to see Torcuil, but there's no need to send him to the shops." I was embarrassed. A healthy young woman, so dependent on others she couldn't even face a supermarket. She couldn't be left alone for a moment in case she did something stupid.

How did this happen?

My gaze went past the loch to the familiar cluster of grey stone that was the Ramsay estate. I couldn't see the stables and the horses from our house, it was too far – there, behind the crest of dark trees, lay the Ramsay stables, such a big part of my lost happiness. I'd loved horseriding. *Before*.

But my greatest loss was just above my head: my attic studio, where I used to work. I hadn't been up there in months.

It weighed on me in a way that was also physical; it hurt so much sometimes I felt I nearly couldn't raise my head.

If someone had told me just a year ago that I would not be drawing any more, that I would be too scared to do so, I would have never believed them.

But this is how I live now.

"I would rather not leave you, you're just back . . ." Angus said.

"Really, Angus. It's okay. I'll dry my hair and tidy up and give the place a clean."

A shadow passed over his face. "You'll exhaust yourself again."

"No, I promise. Honestly. I won't do it . . . that way. Just normal cleaning. Like normal people do." I shrugged and gave a little wan laugh. He didn't even smile. "If you can't even go to the shops, how are you going to manage your place at the RSNO?"

A pause. Cold spread through my bones as I realised what I'd said, the implications of it.

"Good question," he said, and once again he looked away.

My head spun. It was too soon to talk about that; neither of us could have coped.

"Please go to the shops. I promise you I'll be fine. I won't throw myself out of the window or anything." I attempted a laugh. Again, Angus didn't laugh at all.

"I'll do the groceries online."

"Fine," I sighed.

From now on it was going to be like that: he'd check on me, he'd ask me a million times if I were okay. And I couldn't blame him. If he'd tried to do what I'd tried to do, I'd be the same.

All of a sudden, I looked around me and I felt that there was much to do. Everything was out of place and everything needed to be cleaned and sanitised in a way only I knew. My heart was beating too fast again, and my hands felt cold and tingly, the way they did when panic began opening its mouth to swallow me. Too much to do, too much to worry about. And the blackness threatening to engulf me any moment, without warning . . .

I closed my eyes briefly. I needed to tell Emer I was okay.

From Emer88@iol.ie
To Isabel.C.Ramsay@gmail.com
Isabel? Please get in touch. I phoned Angus, and he told me what happened.
Please write. I'm worried sick.
I send you all my love,
Emer x

That was one of no less than fifty emails, imploring me to

get in touch. I felt terrible. No surprises, there – guilt was my default mode.

From Isabel.C.Ramsay@gmail.com
To Emer88@iol.ie
I'm home. I'm okay. Please don't worry about me.
Bell x

A vision from the past flashed in my mind: Angus, Emer, Donal – her best friend – and I camping on a Barra beach, two backpacks of clothes between us, sand everywhere, washing in the freezing sea . . . Donal looking at Emer with such love in his eyes – and still they were just friends, because Emer was in denial. Emer asking us what the sea looked like, telling us that to her the sea was a sound, a scent, and it felt faraway even when she was right on the shore. Emer and I in our flat in Glasgow, when I was at the School of Art and she was studying music – the evenings we spent chatting and drinking cheap cider, Harvey, who was then her guide dog, asleep between us. Emer and I had shared a flat until Angus came on the scene, and Emer, though she would never admit it, was a little bit jealous. 'The two musicians in your life,' she always said.

I switched the computer off, stood up and walked slowly out of the room. I gazed at the metal spiral staircase that led upstairs to my studio.

No.

I wasn't ready.

I just couldn't go back there.

I decided to go downstairs, instead – I felt like I was moving underwater. So much to do, everything to clean and tidy, and I was so tired . . .

81

I looked out at my garden – as always, the sight of it gave me comfort. A blue butterfly was dancing around the rosemary bush, and I looked twice – a butterfly in the winter? To my weary eyes, it seemed like a miracle.

14

Behind the scenes

As I get closer
Closer to you

Isabel

Later, Angus sat in the kitchen while I cooked dinner with what I'd found in the cupboard.

The feeling he was up to something – that he was trying to tell me something, and he was waiting for the right moment – was growing stronger by the minute. This is what happens when you've been married for eight years: you start reading each other's minds. I waited.

"I need to speak to you," he finally said.

"I *knew* it."

"What?"

"I knew you had something to tell me."

"I found someone. For you, I mean."

My stomach knotted. I should have been grateful he was trying to help me, but I was scared, scared that my painstakingly created routine would be upset and that I would have to confront my demons. Terrified of change. Terrified they would make me do things I was terrified of.

Terrified, full stop.

"A therapist? A Skype therapist?" I took a deep breath. "I

might think about it . . ." I said quickly. I knew it'd be no use, but I would do it, if it were asked of me. If it got everyone off my back.

"No, it's not a therapist. You look exhausted, love," he said, stroking my cheek. "Let me make you a cup of tea and then I'll explain."

"I'll make it," I said, filling the kettle while a pot of pasta boiled on the stove. It was all so . . . normal. Like nothing untoward had happened. Like our lives hadn't been turned upside down by what I'd tried to do.

Making dinner. Drinking tea. Quiet domesticity.

And the abyss of my mind ready to open, ready to swallow me.

"You know the way I'll be out for work a lot," Angus began.

"Yes."

"And you'll be on your own."

"Yes. But you think I can't be trusted."

"Well, it's more that . . . I can't relax if I don't know you're okay, and you don't answer the phone, and anyway I can't be texting or emailing, I'll be working . . ."

"But you don't need to worry about me," I said, and the absurdity of it hit me. I'd just tried to swallow enough pills to end it all. But sure, he had nothing to worry about.

How could I convince him I would never try it again? That I would never put him through that again? That I was relieved I was alive?

"Well, I do. I do worry about you. A lot. So Torcuil and I found someone to be with you."

"Here? In this house?" I felt a cold finger travel down my spine. My hands were shaking, all of a sudden.

"Yes. Her name is Clara. She is coming tomorrow . . . She'll just be spending time with you, that's all. See that you are okay."

I turned my back to him, holding the counter with both hands while the kettle clicked. "No."

"Bell . . ."

"I said no!"

"Okay, fine."

"What?"

"I said fine. You don't want strangers in this house, you manoeuvred things so that you wouldn't get visits from the Crisis team or whatever it was called . . . so it'll be me keeping an eye on you. I'm leaving my job."

I turned around to face him. "You can't leave your job! And it's not just a *job*! It's your life!"

"Well, I don't *have* to work for the orchestra. I'll just tell them no, teach music somewhere."

"You can't!"

"Yes, I can. I have to."

"Please don't. I couldn't bear it . . ."

"Then meet this woman."

"This is emotional blackmail!"

"Not exactly. It's just that I love you. It's as simple as that. And I won't leave you alone, not when you're in this state."

Silence. Mutinous on my part, angry on his.

"Bell. I lied for you. So that you could have things your way. Now please will you do this for me!"

"Look. Fine, okay. But only when you're not around. And she is *not* sleeping here."

"She is sleeping here when I'm away with the orchestra, end of! Otherwise I'll stop the trial now."

"Let me at least meet her first!"

"She's coming tomorrow."

"I never had a chance to say no, did I?"

I took a breath, and drank his face in, his voice. His blond-red hair, his eyes, cornflower blue, the straight, determined nose and his long-fingered musician's hands.

I loved him.

"Bell . . ."

"Fine. *Fine*."

"She can come to the house? You'll meet her?"

I love you, Angus, was on the tip of my tongue.

"Bell, please . . ." He seemed exhausted. Oh God, how much I hated all this. How much I hated myself. "Do you have an idea of what you just tried to do? Don't you realise—"

"It was just a *moment*!"

"Isabel! You ended up in hospital." He ran both his hands through his hair, and my heart bled with guilt. He'd called me *Isabel*. To him, I was Bell. He only called me Isabel when he was very angry or very upset.

"Okay. Okay."

"You'll give Clara a chance?"

"Yes. So you don't have to worry about me," I said, more sweetly this time.

"I *always* worry about you."

"One thing, though."

"What?"

"No Skype therapist. It'd be like having to speak into the Eye of Sauron."

He couldn't help smiling a little. "Agreed. But there is something else."

"What?"

"Your medicines. You need to keep the promise you made me at the hospital and start taking them."

"Okay." I said simply. He didn't need to know that panic spread inside me every time I thought about the meds I'd been prescribed, how my father's voice resounded in my ears, cruel, taunting, damning.

He looked at me for a moment, surprised.

"Really?"

"Really," I said, trying to sound convinced. I wasn't lying. I was really determined to do it. Weird. I'd come to the edge of suicide and over, but losing my life didn't seem half as bad as Angus losing his chance to fulfil his dream. Because he deserved it, because he'd given up so much for me. Because he was so talented.

"That is such a relief for me, Bell," he said, and got up to hold me. We were in each other's arms for a long time, and while I snuggled into his chest, his hand stroking my long hair, I felt that maybe I didn't have to fight this battle on my own. That we would fight together, if I allowed him.

Finally, he let me go, and went to open a cupboard.

"They're all here, look." He showed me a bag from Boots. "I got them all for you. The exact doses and when to take them is written on them, see? But I also have a note from the consultant—"

"Well, it's Friday today."

"Saturday. But what does this have to do with anything?"

"There is no point starting things on a Fri— Saturday. I'll start on Monday."

"It makes no sense."

"It makes sense to me."

"You promised me! And you're trying to wriggle out of it

already! I'm sorry, but this is not a matter for discussion. You are going to take your medication!"

"I am! I'll start on Monday."

"Fine! Okay, starting on Monday. Jesus, Bell."

My stomach churned, and the spell of our closeness was over. I wondered how long it would be before he got tired of me. And he should. He should get tired of me, and find someone normal, and get a life. From the window, I saw a whirlpool of dried leaves dancing in our driveway. The season was beginning to turn; the frozen days were on their way. And I would be cold, so cold. I felt tears rolling down my cheeks of their own accord, like my face was melting into tears, and then Angus's arms were around me.

"I love you. I love you," he said over and over and over again.

Later on, while Angus was asleep, I tried.

I tried really hard.

I sat alone, in front of the bag from Boots and a glass of water.

I measured ten drops of a medicine, watching it dissolve into the water.

Then I took a pill from its blister pack and rested it on the kitchen table with trembling hands.

Then the thoughts came.

That they were poison.

That they would make me forget things, and shake, and have terrible nightmares, and turn me into a zombie, or make me so hyper I would not be able to stop rushing from place to place until I collapsed, exhausted. Somewhere inside me, a corner of lucidity told me that the doctor had changed my medication, that those side effects would only be temporary, that if I stuck to it I would feel a lot better.

But the monster inside won.

I poured the drops into the sink and squashed the pill down too, letting the water run to cover the noise of my sobs.

And so there was more lying.

From Isabel.C.Ramsay@gmail.com
To Emer88@iol.ie
Emer. The woman Angus found. She is horrible for sure and I don't want her.

From Emer88@iol.ie
To Isabel.C.Ramsay@gmail.com
You sound like a bratty ten-year-old who doesn't want a new babysitter! Honestly, Isabel, can't you just give her a chance?

From Isabel.C.Ramsay@gmail.com
To Emer88@iol.ie
No.

From Emer88@iol.ie
To Isabel.C.Ramsay@gmail.com
No, you're right. Giving Angus and me a bit of a break from constant worry would be a thoroughly stupid idea.

From Isabel.C.Ramsay@gmail.com
To Emer88@iol.ie
Well, I have accepted anyway because Angus was threatening to leave the orchestra and I can't do this to him.

From Emer88@iol.ie
To Isabel.C.Ramsay@gmail.com
No, you can't. Write to me tomorrow first thing. Tell me all about her. Love you.
Emer xxxxx

From Isabel.C.Ramsay@gmail.com
To Emer88@iol.ie
Love you too. No, really, I do.
Bell x

All these people telling me they love me. They are clearly misguided.

From Isabel.C.Ramsay@gmail.com
To Emer88@iol.ie
I'm sorry for what I did, I began to type. God, how many times would I have to apologise? To how many people? Why, on top of feeling so desperate, did I have to feel guilty too?

Because they loved me.

And I kept letting them down.

I can't explain. I didn't want to die; I just didn't want to feel that way any more. I didn't want to wake up.

I'm glad I did.

While I was under, I had a dream. I saw a woman. I have no idea who she was, but it felt good to be with her, and she led me back. I know it sounds like some stupid eighties series or some weird self-help book, but I think she saved my life.

From Emer88@iol.ie
To Isabel.C.Ramsay@gmail.com
You silly, silly girl. I'm crying as I write this. God, all that matters is that you are alive. What would I do without you? Promise you'll get better. Promise you'll accept help. PROMISE ME!

From Isabel.C.Ramsay@gmail.com
To Emer88@iol.ie
Well, you're still stuck with me, aren't you?
And yes, I promise.
I promise, okay?
Isabel x

From BGiffordblue@gmail.com
To AngusRamsay@gmail.com
Dearest Angus,
Shona told me how hard things are for you right now with your wife's health. I just wanted to let you know that whatever happened, I'll be there. The trial period is not easy, I know, but I'm so sure you'll make it. And like I said, I'm here, for anything.

And I have that book for you. I loved it. Hope to see you soon and give it to you in person.
Bibi xxxx

15

Denial

I shall put
All my songs
In your hands

Isabel

I wasn't always this way.

I'd been a bit melancholy all my life – I suppose it was in the air we breathed at home, seeping off my father like toxic incense – but never to this extent.

I remembered exactly when it started.

Angus and I had spent a wonderful weekend at our friends' in Caithness, John and Zuri. They had a little girl, Amelia, the cutest thing I ever laid my eyes on. We'd spent the weekend hillwalking and playing with Amelia and listening to music – both John and Zuri were musicians and had worked alongside Angus before. It was a happy time.

"She is so cute," I said, stroking Amelia's silky, fine hair. She blew a raspberry, making everyone laugh.

"Can I have a cuddle?" Angus took her gently from me and sat looking into the baby's big, luminous eyes. Up to then, everyone had bounced her, chatted to her, made her laugh, but Angus sat with her quietly, without talking, just holding her and looking into her eyes. Angus had a peace within himself, a sense of stillness and steadiness that always enthralled me, and Amelia felt it too. She lay quietly in his arms, occasionally making a low, sweet sound.

"Someone is feeling broody," joked Zuri.

"Oh, I don't . . ." I protested.

"I think she's talking about Angus!" John said.

Angus smiled and said nothing. To my surprise, I felt a knot in my stomach. I couldn't understand why. What was wrong with me? Why should seeing my husband cuddling a child in such a tender way scare me? But the weird sensation left me as quickly as it had come, and I thought nothing more of it.

And then we came home, and I *unravelled*, just like that.

It had probably been brewing for a while, but it felt so sudden. That night, Angus mentioned the possibility of us having babies – and why not, after all? It seemed like a wonderful idea. It *had* to be a wonderful idea. We were young and brimming with love to give. It was only natural that we should think of children.

"She'll have your eyes, I hope," he said. He's always loved my eyes – a light shade of green – maybe because most people around here have blue eyes.

"And your musical sense."

"Yes, hopefully not yours; the creature wouldn't be able to hold a tune. Not even 'Twinkle Twinkle Little Star'," he said playfully. My lack of musical talent was an ongoing joke between us. At that point, I hit him with a pillow. The future was just in front of us, full of promise. We were in each other's arms, we were talking about a baby and a sliver of new moon was shining above the loch outside our window. I was happy.

I woke up at three in the morning, gasping for air, thinking

I was going to die. All the air had been drawn out of the room and there was no oxygen left. I'd dreamt I'd had a daughter, but I had died, and left her. She was crying alone, desolately, like only babies can – and I couldn't reach her.

I had left her alone, just like my mum had left me.

I slipped out of bed, ran downstairs and sat at the kitchen table for hours, petrified. I was unable to move and unable to draw breath. I must have been breathing, of course, otherwise I'd be dead by now – but it didn't feel like it. I felt like my chest was stuck and would never rise and fall again, like my lungs would never fill again.

I cried tears of terror. I had no idea what was happening to me. I was drenched in sweat, freezing in the cold night air, the house silent and dark and still. Something in me had snapped. I had been confined to a lonely, faraway moon circling at the edge of space. I was on my own, in a place of dread.

That was how it began.

And then it got worse.

16

Love, long ago

I look for her
Like Orpheus seeks Euridice
Leading her out
The world of the dead

Angus
If you'd known Bell before she got ill, you wouldn't believe it was the same person. The Bell I fell in love with was sunny and full of joy. She was brave, and funny, and irresistible.

We grew up together, in a way. Although her father was Irish and they lived in Ireland, they came to spend the summers in Glen Avich to see Bell's aunt, her dad's sister. I was in boarding school, then at university, but I always tried to catch her when I was around. I had a crush on her even when we were children. But Bell began going out with my brother, and then I found out it was serious. They were engaged. I came home less and less. Maybe I didn't want to see them together, I don't know.

But one Christmas, something happened. *We* happened, Bell and I.

I was home from university for the Christmas holidays. My father was bedridden, so I spent most of the first few days in his room. I played for him, and I could see he was proud of me.

Torcuil took advantage of my presence to spend more time with Bell, out for windy walks around the loch or at the Green Hat, away from our family's heavy presence.

Every once in a while, this girl I was seeing rang me; I did my best not to answer the phone. The signal was bad; I was busy; I was with my parents. It just wasn't working out. I said to myself that I was too young for a serious relationship, that all I wanted was to play my music.

I believed it.

One night, I was playing for some friends and family, and *she* was there. Her cheeks were burning, and what I remember the most were her eyes, green like spring leaves: she couldn't stop looking at me, and I couldn't stop looking at her.

I knew. I knew I would not be able to resist. But that didn't mean I wouldn't try with all I had.

I looked away. I went for a walk through frozen fields and sat at the edge of the loch, in silence.

Bell. Bell. I called her Bell in my heart, though she was "Isabel" when I said it aloud.

To Torcuil, she was Izzy.

Oh, show me the way to go home.

Bell, show me the way to go home.

And then she was there, beside me. When our eyes locked, we both knew it was too late to stop, it was impossible to turn back.

We tried, both of us, and we couldn't help it, but we fell into each other.

Hope thwarted will make you sick. Love unfulfilled will make you sick. Not to be with each other, not to touch each other, was poison for us. We could not survive apart. We could not live in a world of things that might have been.

But for Torcuil's sake, we had to try.

Everybody realised, of course. What was happening between Bell and I was plain to see. We were both ashamed; I left Glen Avich at the end of the holidays, early in the morning, with a rushed goodbye to my parents. I did not say goodbye to Bell; I did not say goodbye to Torcuil.

I wanted to leave them both behind, as far as I could go. Bell, because I loved her; Torcuil, because I had hurt him. I had broken my brother's trust.

Bell turned up at my flat in Glasgow three days later, in tears. She'd dissolved the engagement to Torcuil. She said she couldn't lie.

"You wouldn't be lying. You love him," I said.

"It's not him I love."

The weight of her words fell on me like something terrible, like something beautiful. Like salvation.

Eight months later, we got married.

When we were both twenty-two, we moved back to Glen Avich – Bell would work as a freelance illustrator; I would continue my nomadic musician's life. I would practise my violin while she drew, and I thought our happiness would never end.

And then, all of a sudden, she became ill.

It was sudden, yes, but it got worse slowly.

I wished I could tell everyone how she used to be – a little spark of joy and life, with an Irish accent and a deep, deep passion for art.

Her smile was a field of daisies.

So that was Bell. Fearless, joyful and ready to embrace life. Not the shell she'd become.

I knew all about her childhood of course, how she didn't speak to her father now and only seldom to her sister – they'd been a surly, silent presence at our wedding – but I didn't think that one day all she'd been through would catch up with her in such a terrible way.

It's difficult to pinpoint exactly when it started – when my wife became a nervous, shaky shadow of herself. I remember her having a panic attack one night after a day out with friends, but that's about it. It was gradual, until she couldn't get out of the house any more, and I didn't have my Bell any more, and nothing was right any more.

Sometimes I thought she was like Briar Rose, asleep under a curse. And I hoped, I prayed my kiss would wake her up one day.

17

A world without you

And suddenly there was
A world without you

Torcuil

Of course, I knew what was happening. I just didn't want to believe it. Izzy disappeared for a couple of days – her aunt said she wasn't at home, but I knew she was. I nearly didn't want to speak to her, I was so afraid.

My father knew as well. It was strange how, though he was bedridden and pretty much always stuck in his bedroom, he was always aware of what was going on. My mother was busy with other things.

After three sleepless nights, Izzy came to the house and she told me she couldn't marry me.

I said of course, we were very young, we could take it slow.

No, she said, *I can't marry you, and I can't be with you.*

As she spoke, her words fell on me and washed away; I couldn't listen, I couldn't let them sink in. It was too cruel; it couldn't possibly be true.

Not my brother.

Not Izzy.

She cried, of course. I thought it was a bit late for crying.

I thought I wanted to comfort her because she was upset. I thought I hated her.

I loved her.

I'd like to say I kept my dignity, but I didn't: I begged with all I had, and then over the next few weeks I phoned her all the time. She would always answer, always be there to take my pain, my rage, my failed attempts at reasoning. I believe she felt she deserved to be punished. That she *had* to listen to my protestations and my pain. I wrote her long, meandering letters that I never sent, and watched them turn to ash in my fireplace.

I never spoke to Angus, not once.

I stopped phoning Izzy too.

There was silence for almost a year, the longest year of my life. Angus and Isabel got married during that time. It was a lucky, lucky coincidence I was invited to a history conference in Munich, so I had a good enough excuse not to attend the ceremony. If people thought it was strange that I should choose to attend a conference instead of my brother's wedding, nobody mentioned it. I could just picture it: me, the best man, my heart bleeding all over my white shirt while my brother married the love of my life. Now that would have made for a nice party.

Then my father died, and Angus and I embraced, in tears, over his grave.

The rift was mended; my heart was not.

18

Wrench

What is good for me
Hurts more than what is bad

Isabel

I saw them coming from my bedroom window, walking up the path and then disappearing along the back wall, towards the kitchen entrance. My heart skipped and jumped. For a moment I thought, absurdly, that I would not answer.

I ran downstairs and, on impulse, bolted the door.

Then I unbolted it. I couldn't lock my husband out. But surely I could lock a stranger out? I bolted it again and ran upstairs, panicked.

"We're here! Can Clara come in?" Angus called. He must have tried to open the door and found it locked.

I went to sit on top of the stairs and looked out of the bars, like a shy child when visitors arrive at the house.

"No," I said, though I cringed at how childish it made me seem. How childish I actually was. This whole illness had made me revert to being a frightened child, in a way.

"Isabel? It's Clara. Please, can I come in and see you?"

I froze. It was a familiar voice, but I couldn't quite place it. I stood immobile, shaking. "Isabel?" she repeated, and suddenly I remembered.

A hazy recollection floated by – lying in my bed, still under the effect of the pills, and the woman stroking my hair. How could it be?

Suddenly, though most of me was terrified – a stranger at the door waiting to come in – part of me was *curious*. A little part of me.

But it couldn't be possible.

Angus and I had established it had been a dream, and someone from a dream couldn't possibly be standing at my door.

"Look, we're on the doorstep," Angus called. "Please, come and open the door."

I couldn't resist the plea in my husband's voice, and the sheer shame of the whole situation overwhelmed me. What would the woman think? That I was deranged.

A side effect of my illness: humiliation.

"Are you okay?" the woman called again, and again I trembled inside.

I walked downstairs, slowly, and unlocked the door.

"Yes. I'm fine," I said, peeking from the stairs. She was wearing jeans and a cobalt-blue top, and her brown hair was folded on top of her head.

"Is it a bad time?" she asked, a warm smile on her face. Really, genuinely *warm*, like she was happy to see me. I couldn't help responding to it, so I smiled back and, to my surprise, my lips actually stretched. A successful smile. Something that hadn't happened in a long while.

"I think you were in my dream," I said.

Angus looked from me to the woman as I slowly opened the door further.

"What dream?" Angus asked.

"Remember? I told you. The woman I saw. I think . . . No, it can't be. Sorry," I said to Clara, and I blushed. That was absurd. And she'd think I was delusional, on top of everything else.

Once again, Angus looked from me to Clara. I think he was at a loss for words. I had just said that someone from a dream had walked out of my mind and was now standing in my hall. Maybe he thought I really was losing it.

"Sorry," I repeated.

I had been delirious when I dreamt of that woman, my blood full of chemical poison. I couldn't even remember her features.

But I could remember her words.

"Bell? Can we go to the kitchen and make some coffee for Clara?"

Angus stood beside me, while Clara hovered outside the door; Clara would not stop smiling like she was bursting with joy – was she really *so* happy to see me? I stood awkwardly, uncertain as to what to do next, unable to make small talk. Being terrified of going out and terrified of letting people in, I hadn't talked much to anyone in a couple of years; I had forgotten how to. I wanted to let her in and close the door, but I was frightened to actually have her inside the house. A cold breeze was blowing in.

Clara read my mind.

"If you'd rather not let me in, it's fine, really, we can have a chat here."

"Oh. Yes. Sorry. It's just . . ."

"She—" Angus began to explain, but Clara interrupted

him, looking me straight in the eye. Like this was something between me and her.

It felt good. It felt empowering. That for once I was being treated like an adult with a will of her own, not like an invalid that needed to be taken charge of.

"I understand. Really. Are you cold?" she asked thoughtfully.

"A bit. You?"

Angus's gaze was still moving between us during this conversation he had no part of. Things were clearly going differently from how he had thought. Well, how could I have predicted that the person chosen by him to keep an eye on me had come out of a dream?

"No. But if you are, maybe I could step in and close the door?"

"Of course, sorry," I said, and let her in, and closed the door, and for a moment it simply felt like the sensible thing to do, before my fears got in the way and started screaming at me.

There she was, inside my house. And I wasn't shaking, I wasn't panicking.

"Please don't worry, I'm happy to stay here," Clara said. "We can go at your pace."

But standing on the doormat, even with the door closed, felt silly.

"No, it's okay. Come in. Would you like a cup of tea? Margherita sent some biscuits. *Biscotti*, she calls them. You're staying with them, aren't you?"

"Yes. I'm renting their cottage. It's lovely," she said, following me into the kitchen.

Angus's eyeballs were about to fall out. I was pretty surprised too. But hey, I would just go with it, until panic took over. Like it always did.

"Please sit down," I said, and Angus rushed to move the chair for her, as if I would change my mind any moment, while I assembled a teabag and a mug the right way, without upsetting the order in my kitchen and sending me into a spiral of anxiety.

We sat and drank our tea, and it was surreal.

"So, I understand you'll come and keep an eye on me."

"Clara will—" Angus started, but she interrupted him. Again.

"Yes. I'll come and keep you company. So you won't be alone while Angus is away."

She made it sound nearly sensible. Or acceptable, anyway.

"I haven't been well."

"Yes."

"So I'm alone a lot."

"I know."

"People have been saying to me to just pull myself together. But I can't."

"I *know*," she repeated, with emphasis. I got the feeling she really understood. "If you're okay with me coming to keep you company, we can think of things to do. Or I can just leave you alone to do your thing. Think about it, and you can let me know."

I nodded.

"Did you draw those?" She gestured to the framed illustrations on the kitchen wall.

"Yes."

"They are *so* beautiful."

"You're just saying that."

"No. They really are wonderful. Angus, you must feel so proud of Isabel."

"I am," he said, with such love in his eyes it was a stab in the heart. Because I was letting him down in that too.

"I haven't worked in so long. I feel so . . . *dry*."

"But it won't be forever. You'll get better . . ." she said, but I wasn't listening any more.

Obviously, I can't have Clara here . . . She is not Angus or Morag and therefore she is not allowed, something terrible will happen if I let her in. I'll have to sit with her by my side, trying to block out the terror of having someone in my house, of breathing the same air as her. Maybe I'll succeed, and I maybe I could grow to like her, but then she'll hurt me, or get depressed like me and kill herself and I'll be left alone . . .

"Will you show me more of your work one day?" Somewhere in my mind, her words registered and my answer surprised me.

"Okay," I heard myself saying.

My voice was like a bell above the din of a busy hall, the voices of my fears, crazy, cruel, irrational, struggling to drown it.

"Really?"

"Yes. I will show you," I said, trying to smile, but this time it didn't work. I was too scared to smile. What had I just done? I felt sick.

"That's great, thank you!" She clasped her hands together in a gesture that was nearly childish. I noticed she had a spattering of freckles on her nose and that her eyes were so green in the bright light of the kitchen.

"Right. I'll let you be. I'll come back then . . ." She seemed suddenly unsure, as if she feared me taking it back, and she got up to leave.

"Yes. Please do," I added, and once again, I was infinitely

106

surprised at the fact that I meant it. "But wait, don't go. You haven't finished your tea . . ."

She smiled. "I'll stay another few minutes, then."

Angus had been looking at us, following the conversation like an outsider. Now I think he wanted to make sure things were settled, so he spoke.

"Bell, Clara will stay with you when I can't. She will sleep here as well, in the guest room."

"To keep you company," Clara added.

"To watch me," I said.

"Bell . . ."

"It's fine. Really."

"Really?" Angus couldn't believe how the whole thing had gone. And I couldn't either.

I nodded. Clara finished her tea and her *biscotto*, then she stood up to go. "I'll see you tomorrow, then. At . . ." She looked at Angus.

"I'll be leaving for Glasgow around half six in the morning."

"No problem, I'll be here in good time. Bye, Isabel," she said simply.

"Bye," I could only say, as if my whole life hadn't shifted.

As if everything was still the same, when it wasn't.

I watched her from the window, and I waved. I watched her walk away, stepping in between two wings of rose plants, slow and deliberate like a queen. I noticed a blue butterfly fluttering behind her, following her like a bride's train.

"So that went well," Angus said cheerily as he stepped back into the kitchen, but he sounded a bit brittle.

"Yes."

"So . . . you'll be showing her your work?"

"I don't know if I can," I shrugged. "I haven't been up there in ages." I looked up to the ceiling.

"You do your thing, okay? Take your time," he said softly, and I looked into his handsome face, those eyes so clear and steadfast, the five o'clock shadow of a tired man.

"Okay."

"And Bell?"

"Mmm?"

"I love you."

"I love you too. More than anything," I said, but I couldn't look at him in the eye, because I felt so ashamed of myself at saying such a thing. I loved him, and yet I had put him through something so terrible.

Still. On Monday all would change, because I'd start to take my medication and all would get better.

"Everyone wants you to feel better, Isabel. Everyone roots for you."

And I'm so scared I'll let you all down, I thought.

I kept my face hidden in his chest, where it was safe, and he braided his hands together on my back, to keep me inside the cocoon of his love.

I sat on the stairs to think. It was a favourite place of mine, since I was a little girl. Like a neutral zone where I could escape my father's silence and my sister's anger. I played with my hair as I reflected on all that had happened. I hadn't been to the hairdresser in over a year, so my hair hung long and lank down past my shoulders. I thought it looked sad, but Angus loved it; he said it was like a cascade of silk. Everything that was wrong about me, he made it sound like it was *right*.

And yes, I would try to get better for him. I would take my medication. On Monday morning, at eight o'clock, I would sit there and take all my drops and pills, like the doctor had said.

For Angus.

And maybe a little bit for myself too.

The winding road

The irresistible march
Of things that change

Torcuil

I left little Leo with Lara while I went for some groceries, and then I decided to stop at La Piazza to say hello to Margherita and maybe give her a hand. That was, if she'd let me. She was pretty territorial around her kitchen, maybe because I tended to be useless at cooking, like everyone in my family. Or maybe because it was something just for herself, away from me and away from her children, her own space to be something other than a partner and a mother. I understood very well how she felt. I was longing to go back to the university and back to an everyday routine, with no more emergencies, no more jumping if the mobile rang, in fear of bad news. Just . . . normality. To be with my students and my papers seemed an oasis of peace in comparison with how life in Glen Avich had been. I had taken a few days off last week to be near if Angus needed me, but I would be back at work tomorrow. Much as it pained me to admit it, I was looking forward to it.

He'd phoned me earlier to say that he and Bell were going to spend the day alone at home – he wanted to gauge how her time with Clara had been and help her to accept Clara's new role in her life, as well as just having some peaceful time together. I remembered a time when this would have broken my heart: years ago, when I was still in love with Izzy and desperately trying to deny it – long, unhappy years, until Margherita swept away the last remains of heartache.

On my way to the coffee shop I looked back at that time with dismay, and relief that it was over. I'd probably erased most of that era from my mind, but there were things from the time just after Izzy had left me for Angus that I could never forget. I couldn't forget that my eyes were dry, my heart was shut, and I was drifting away on a lonely sea. I had watched my father die slowly while I was cut off from my brother and a stranger to my sister and my mother.

Without Izzy.

I used to close my eyes at night and imagine Izzy coming back to me, and in the little films I played to myself I took her back without question, forgave her without resentment, loved her without reserve, like it could never happen again. During the day, I said to myself I was over her; at night, I was raw with longing. Even after Angus and I made up, after my father's death; even as "Bell and Angus" became a way to address one single creature, like one could not go without the other; even then, I still loved her.

It was easy to convince everyone I was over her. It was easy for someone like me, who carries his feelings buried deep inside anyway, to pretend. My love for her was buried so deep that nobody could see it any more – at times, not even me. Buried like a lost jewel at the bottom of a black, black loch.

Sometimes I believed my own lie and acted like nothing had happened; sometimes I was sure I would never recover. I went through my life on autopilot, breathing in, breathing out, putting one foot in front of the other, eating and sleeping automatically, because it was necessary for survival. All this made worse by Angus's and Izzy's choice to move back to Glen Avich and buy the cottage on the other side of the loch, which had stood empty for a long time. We had made peace, we were close again, so why not? I had been so good at hiding my true feelings, so thorough in deleting all traces of love and loss from the surface of my mind, that Angus could not suspect how seeing them doing up their house under my nose broke my heart. I couldn't take it any more and took on a lecturing post in London. After my father's death, nothing tied me to Glen Avich – or so I wanted to believe.

After a few years I came back, of course. Contrary to what I thought, I pined for Ramsay Hall and Glen Avich. I was surprised how seeing Angus and Izzy together – Isabel, she was now *Isabel* – hurt a little bit less. How I could live with it. Just.

But all this was long ago. Everything changed once again, with Margherita and her children coming into my life.

And here I was, a partner and a stepfather – who would have imagined I would be doing nursery runs, standing among the playground mums and dads, holding Leo's hand while we waited to step in? And helping Lara to do her homework in the evening?

I was sitting at the window table at La Piazza with a steaming coffee in front of me, watching rain splash on the cars and gather in puddles on the pavement. Debora was sparkling with energy and cheerfulness, as ever. If only I could take a little bit of her and Margherita's eternal positive mood and pour it inside Izzy like a healing balm . . .

"Any news of Isabel?" Debora asked softly, as if reading

112

my thoughts, and her forehead creased in concern. The shop was empty but for a few pensioners near the fireplace, so there were no curious ears to listen, and Debora had showed her kindness towards Izzy many times, so I was happy to reply. I usually felt protective of Izzy, quite unwilling to share news of her.

"She's a lot better, thank you . . ." I began. And then I saw Clara from the window, strolling towards the cafe as if she were on a sunny promenade, as if the icy rain didn't bother her at all. She came in with a warm smile and a gust of cold air, trailing a soaking umbrella with her. After greeting Debora and the girls she sat with me with a murmured 'May I?' I waited until her order was on the table so we could speak freely, without being overheard. When Angus and I had spoken on the phone earlier, he'd been unable to tell me about Izzy and Clara's first encounter – apart from a laconic *it was fine* – because Izzy was there. I needed to know more.

"How did it go?" I asked at once. There was no need to specify what I was talking about.

"It went well. She is such a lovely person . . ." There was a light in Clara's eyes, like she was genuinely happy to spend her time with Izzy, and for a moment I was jealous. It was so hard for me to keep in touch with Izzy, to know what she was doing, what she was thinking – but she let a stranger into her life so easily? But then I cringed at my unfairness.

"She let you in okay?" I asked, and I didn't just mean into her home.

"Well, after a little while. We had cup of tea and a chat. I think it's going to work out," she said, and she was beaming.

"Good morning," an Irish voice came from the kitchen, before I could say anything else. Aisling walked through from behind the counter, followed by a tiny girl with the face of a mouse and a mane of blue hair. "Hi guys, this is my sister, Kate. At last. I can go home and put my feet up," she said, patting her belly.

"I'll show her the ropes. You're officially on maternity leave, so go home or go and sit on the sofa and I'll bring you a cup of tea," Debora said.

"Are you sure?" Aisling didn't seem at ease with being served instead of doing the serving.

"Absolutely. Can I get you something else, Torcuil? Clara?"

"No thanks, I just had a gallon of coffee," I said.

"You can never have enough caffeine in my view," Margherita appeared from the kitchen. "Hi, Clara. Was Leo okay?" she asked me.

"He was great. Went without any bother. I thought maybe I could give you a hand?"

"No, you're fine, chat away." She dismissed me with a wave of her hand. Just like I thought, she would not let me near the food she was preparing. She gave me a peck on the cheek and disappeared again.

"Kate, if you come here I'll show you how to work the coffee machine . . ." Debora began. At that moment, a loud song pierced our ears.

"Sorry, it's just my phone! I've got to get this. It's Pablo," Kate declared, and strode out of the coffee shop into the street.

Aisling and Debora looked at each other.

"Wait, I'll just clear up that table . . ."

"You go *home*!" Debora ordered. "Or if you want to stay, you are going to sit there and eat cake. You are forbidden to do any work! Enough is enough."

"Fine," Aisling said, and gazed out of the window at her

114

sister, who was standing close to the wall, out of the rain, and talking on her mobile. Clara and I exchanged an amused look.

"Go sit on the sofas," Debora said.

"I wouldn't get up again!"

"Come and sit beside me, then," Debora said, patting the chair behind the counter.

"Sorry!" Kate walked in again. "That was my fiancée."

Fiancée? She looked about fifteen.

"Fiancée?" Aisling got up again. "Do Mum and Dad know about this?"

"Not yet. So don't tell them."

"Kate, you are still—"

"I'm old enough to make my own decisions!"

"Right. We'll talk about it later," Aisling concluded and gave her a *wait till I get my hands on you* kind of look.

"Anyway, Kate, come and I'll show you how to use the coffee machine—" Debora began again.

"Ouch!" Kate said, bringing her hand to her eye.

"What's wrong?"

"My contact lens fell out. I can't see a thing without it. I need to go home and get my glasses."

Debora and Aisling looked at each other again as Kate disappeared out of the shop once more.

"I'm going to kill her!" Aisling said, and disappeared after her. It was like being at the theatre, really. But with all the commotion, I hadn't had the chance to speak to Clara, and she was already standing to leave.

"Well, I'm off. I'll see you soon. And don't worry, it'll be fine," she said.

I didn't have time to say anything but "Keep me posted", and she was already out of the coffee shop with a hurried goodbye. It was like she didn't want to give away too much, somehow. I wondered why.

I watched Clara leave, walking down the street with the umbrella in her hand, closed, and the rain soaking her hair. She seemed immune to the cold. I was about to stand and go home too when a black-haired woman came in. I was so rarely in the village, I had forgotten how you're bound to meet someone you know at every corner.

It was Anne, my former classmate at Glen Avich Primary and then Kinnear High. She was a good friend of Isabel; they had always played together during her summers in Glen Avich, and then, as teenagers, they went out with the same group of friends. I watched while she slipped her umbrella into the vase beside the door and then walked to the counter, her spine straight. She was a heavyset girl, with black hair and freckles all over her fair skin. She carried a sense of peace and contentment about her, with her unrushed ways and slow, deliberate voice.

"What do you have in the way of cake, Debora? It's my father-in-law's birthday and we're throwing a bit of a bash," she said, tucking a strand of black hair, streaked with grey, behind her ear. It was strange to think she was the same age as Izzy – she looked a lot older. Izzy had, somehow, stayed frozen in time. But Anne also looked so much happier than Izzy.

"Anything you dream of and more," Debora replied with a smile. "I can make you a sponge and decorate it for him, if you have time to wait until tomorrow?"

"I'm afraid I have to take what you have ready. It's all very last-minute. The party is tonight . . . Oh, hello, Torcuil!"

"Hi Anne, how are you? And the family?" Anne had four boys and a huge extended family that usually trailed after her.

I realised it was the first time I'd ever seen her on her own, without either a child or a granny or two in tow.

"All good, thank you. Debora, could I have that chocolate cake, please? And a latte? Do you mind if I sit with you, Torcuil?"

"Please do." She did, resting her shopping bags on the floor.

"I was just wondering how is Isabel . . ."

"Well, she had a bit of a blip . . ." I didn't want to talk about Izzy behind her back, but Anne was a good friend, and I didn't want her to feel unwelcome about asking after Izzy. I was happy she had. In spite of Izzy's effort to isolate herself over the last three years, there were people all around who cared for her, thought of her, wished her well. I thought it was a precious thing; I thought she needed to know it was so.

"I know. I heard."

Of course she had.

"Yes." I looked into my coffee.

"How is she now?"

"She's back at home. That's something."

"Oh, Torcuil, my heart goes out to her. I tried to get in touch, but she never seemed to want to talk . . ."

"She doesn't mean it. It's just . . ."

"You don't need to say. I just want Isabel to know I'm here if she needs me. I'll be here when she's better."

"Thank you. She'll be happy to hear that."

"I made a parcel for her a wee while ago – some soaps. I left it with Angus. I'll make her another one."

"I'm sure she'll appreciate it," I said, and I thought of how people sent Isabel packages and letters, as if she was marooned somewhere far, far away.

"I just wanted to say . . ." It was her turn to look down, now. "Sometimes, my husband . . . Well, my husband went through a stage when he wasn't really feeling himself. Dr Robertson gave him some stuff to take and he felt a lot better."

"Yes. Thank you," I said. A silent brotherhood and sisterhood of sorrow. I was grateful.

"Will you give her my love?"

"Of course."

She looked at me thoughtfully, like she wanted to say something else. But then she changed her mind and left, clutching her cake box to her chest, her dark-green umbrella bobbing as she walked under the freezing rain. On impulse, I took my mobile out and texted Angus.

Could you give Isabel a message from me? Tell her that Anne was asking after her, she sends her love.

Any lifeline Izzy was thrown was worth clutching.

20

Respite

Keep me close, keep me
In the shelter of your arms

Isabel

Angus and I were alone, at home. It happened so rarely that when it did I treasured every moment, every hour. We lay together until late, the curtains drawn, under the warm, heavy duvet. In his arms, I found an oasis of peace, a moment of respite from my restless thoughts. I couldn't even remember the last time we'd been alone together without arguing or discussing my health.

It was like a miracle, and I was determined not to spoil it with anxieties or upset. All I wanted to do was lie in his arms, listening to his steady heartbeat, and forget all about the world.

"So, it went okay with Clara, didn't it?" he said in a low, soft voice, caressing my hair. We were so close that I could hear his voice resound in his chest.

I nodded. I didn't want to speak. Not yet.

"You think it will work out with her?

I nodded again.

"You seemed to be so relaxed with her. I have to admit, I was surprised."

"So was I," I whispered.

"I can't begin to tell you my relief. Thank you, Bell—"

"Please don't thank me. Don't."

"You pushed yourself so that I could still go to work. I'm so grateful. I really am."

I couldn't believe what he was saying. He was *grateful*? After all I had inflicted on him?

His love for me always left me speechless. His unconditional, generous kindness towards me was a treasure I would not squander, I would not relinquish.

He placed a kiss on my temple and I closed my eyes, drinking in his love, his presence, his warmth. He wrapped his arms around me and began kissing me, and I forgot all about the darkness inside me and lost myself in him.

Afterwards, he brought me a cup of coffee and opened the curtains. I brought my knees to my chest and sipped my hot, sugared coffee while he sat on the windowsill and looked outside. Autumn was singing its last, spectacular song before the land fell asleep for a long, long time.

21

The memory of colours

And in my dreams I bathed
In purple and yellow
And in my dreams I was
The rainbow

Isabel

Finally it was Monday, and another week was starting. I wasn't that nervous the first time Clara came *officially*, without Angus. Well, maybe a little.

Okay, I was *very* nervous. Nearly panicky, but not quite, though I could feel my heart beating through my T-shirt. But the first meeting had been good, so that boded well.

She arrived a few minutes before Angus left, at break of dawn. He opened the door, all ready and packed to drive away, and Clara *tiptoed* into the house, smoothly, after a brief whispered exchange with my husband. Not literally, of course – but if *felt* like she was tiptoeing. She slipped in like a guest, without a hint of bossiness, without making me feel she was there to watch me, to check on me. In fact, she was nearly timid. I had been dreading that she would start telling me what to do, watch that I take my medicines – that would have been a problem – watch me eating, act like some sort of nurse. Which was what she was, but I preferred to forget about it.

But she did none of this. She didn't act like I had to somehow report to her. She sat with me in the kitchen, silent and smiling, a calm presence that asked for nothing. I thought I was going to have to do my best to avoid her, maybe even barricade myself in my bedroom and try to forget she was there, but I sat at the table in front of her and we were like two pieces of a jigsaw slotting together.

Strange.

"It's awfully early. Fancy a coffee? I'll make it, if it's okay?" she said.

"There is some ready . . ." I said, gesturing at the cafetière. I got up before her. I preferred taking charge in my own kitchen. I poured us both a coffee and lay milk and sugar on the table, like I'd done this with her forever. Like she wasn't a stranger sitting with me at half past six in the morning. And then I wiped everything the way I liked it. The way I *needed* it. I had a million little rituals that kept me prisoner, and if I didn't follow them I would go into a panic.

"It must be weird, having me at the house so early," she said, reading my mind.

"It's weird to have *anyone* at the house," I replied, wrapping my cardigan tighter around myself. "At pretty much any time."

"I can imagine. It's good of you to let me come. Thank you," she said, and the conversation was so surreal I didn't know what to say next.

"So, what's the plan for today?" she went on.

"I don't know. I usually . . . I don't know. I hang around. I clean and tidy, mainly. I don't do much." I used to work all day, day in and day out. I loved it that way. To lose myself in my art. But not any more.

"I don't want to be intrusive . . . I mean, it must be strange enough to have me around . . . but Angus said you'd start taking your medicines today?"

"I did! I did already. Before you arrived," I lied quickly.

"Oh, that's good. Listen, I was thinking . . . will you show me your studio? Angus said you have an amazing room up in the attic. And I'd love to learn more about art."

"I haven't been up there in ages," I said curtly, and began playing with my hair.

"Oh. Sorry."

"It's just . . . I don't know. I told you. Nothing comes out. I tried to draw and paint and I just couldn't. So I stopped."

Clara looked at me sympathetically. "Well, they talk about writer's block . . . you have artist's block. It will all come back," she said softly.

"Do you think so?" I asked, and then I immediately felt angry with myself. I was seeking reassurance from a total stranger. Why was I doing that?

"Of course. It's just that you're not well, right now. It won't be forever."

Really?

At that moment, I realised I had come to be quite sure my illness would last forever, in spite of what Angus always believed, always told me: that one day I would magically be the person I used to be.

But maybe, like many illnesses, it would simply go away, one day. Some become chronic, but some just . . . *go.*

Maybe there was hope.

I gazed at my pictures, framed and displayed all around the kitchen – colourful paintings of owls and deer and foxes, all with a magical quality to them, in a style that was somewhere between realistic and primitive – my style. My signature. It was how I had made a name for myself, how I had slowly, slowly built a career. With my soul's work.

22

What I leave behind

What I leave behind
Is my heart itself

Angus

It was all a big exercise in trust, wasn't it? To leave Bell behind, believe that Clara would take good care of her, believe that she would keep herself safe and not do anything stupid. We'd spent yesterday together and it had been perfect. Twenty-four hours of peace, like a butterfly's life.

The drive to Glasgow was full of thoughts of Isabel, and how torn I was between her and my job. Somehow, between Glen Avich and the city, the wrench happened and my thoughts turned to music. It was never easy, but it worked; it had to work. If I was to juggle Bell's illness and the orchestra, the wrench *had* to happen.

When I got into rehearsal, Bibi was the first to greet me, leaving the group to come and say hello. She was very ... expansive, when it came to me. I wasn't sure how to take it. On the other hand, she was like that with Kyoko too, the Japanese cello player who was on trial with me, so maybe it was my imagination running away.

"Hi! I have that book we talked about. It's in my bag, I'll just get it ..."

"Oh, thanks. You didn't have to."

"It's no problem. There," she said, and swept her dark hair away from her face. "It's great to see you. How have you been?"

"I'm good, you?"

"Great! Listen, I found this place off Sauchiehall Street, why don't you and me make a run for it at break and get a quiet lunch?"

"I . . ."

I was saved by the conductor calling us to start.

It was weird to be away from Bell, but when I started playing I forgot about everything. And no, that's not to say I stopped caring, or I stopped carrying Bell in my heart every moment. It was a different thing. When I played, I wasn't myself any more: I was music.

I lost myself in it and my heart had only one reason to beat. It's difficult to explain if you haven't felt it: it was like suspending time, a perfect harmony of body and soul and the rest of the universe. Like being immortal. Immersed in beauty and bliss.

That was what music did to me.

It didn't always feel good. It was also an obsession. A hard mistress who wanted me to give her pretty much everything I was and everything I had. Sometimes music was freedom; sometimes she tied me with more binds than I could ever imagine, and I realised I wasn't her master, I was her slave. Sometimes I looked at my violin and thought of all the hours I practised, and how my work was never finished, never quite good enough, never perfect, and I realised as much as I loved it, I hated it too.

Rehearsals were over, and we sat on the small couches against the wall, drinking coffee. I looked out of the window at the pouring rain, and I wondered if it was raining in Glen Avich. I wondered how Bell and Clara are getting on.

I wondered if I would ever have my Bell back.

"You are lost in thought," a voice said beside me. It was Bibi.

"Yes. Just . . . lots on my mind."

"Your wife?" she whispered. She looked at me like she knew everything there was to know about me. I nodded, taken aback. We hardly knew each other, really, and she was already asking me personal questions. The orchestra was a small fishpond, a tiny Glen Avich where news got around fast and everybody knew each other's business, but usually it wasn't spoken aloud so brazenly.

"Why don't we go somewhere for proper coffee" – she gestured at the instant stuff I had poured for myself – "and a quiet chat? I'm a good listener." I supposed she'd given up on lunch and was now settling for coffee.

"But I'm not much of a talker," I replied. Her face fell, and suddenly I felt cruel. She meant well – she just wanted to offer a sympathetic ear and some support. The problem was, it might have been what I needed – sympathy and support – but it didn't mean I was going to accept it.

"Sorry, that wasn't nice. Of course. Let's go. Kyoko around?"

"She's making a call home."

It had to be just us, then.

We sat in the cafe around the corner and I noticed how blue Bibi's eyes were – forget-me-not blue. They were a bit bulgy though, a bit manic, I mused, and then berated myself for such an unkind thought. Bell's eyes were deep green, and they had these brown specks in them, so unique . . .

127

"So, how long have you been in the orchestra?" I asked, to break the silence.

"Oh, four years now. A long time . . . for me." She laughed. "Actually I was thinking of leaving, but then . . ."

"What happened?"

Bibi shrugged. "I changed my mind. I decided it's worth staying."

"Where are you from, exactly?"

"Tennessee. I thought my accent would give me away!" She laughed again. She laughed a lot, but not in an irritating way. More like cheery. Full of life. She had a generous mouth and curls that bounced when she spoke animatedly, punctuating her words.

"I can't really tell American accents apart."

"You're from a small village around here, aren't you?"

"Well, not exactly around here, a few hours' drive away."

"That's around here, by American standards." Again, that lively laugh.

"It's near Aberdeen. Tiny place."

"What's the name?"

"Glen Avich," I said, and just saying it aloud conjured the scent of wind, the still loch, the pine-covered, silent mountains. Home. Always.

"Glen Avick."

I smiled. "Avich!"

"That's what I said! Avick! Avi . . . ch! No, I can't say it! So," she said, her long, fine fingers braided around her cup, "are you enjoying the orchestra?"

"I'm loving every minute, to be honest."

"Are you? Because you look so preoccupied . . ."

"Well, that has nothing to do with the job. It's . . . other things."

"Tell me. What's on your mind?" she said, taking a sip of her coffee.

"Well, nothing . . . Just stuff at home."

"Your wife?"

I nodded.

"What's wrong with her, if I may ask?"

You may not.

"Oh, she's just a bit down on herself. She'll get better."

"Of course," she said, and just for a second, she rested her hand on mine. "Everything will be fine."

I froze. And then, to my great surprise, I realised it didn't feel that bad. It didn't feel that bad to see that someone other than Torcuil and Margherita actually care. To see that when I was in Glasgow, working, there was someone who knew what was going on.

"Thank you, Bibi," I said, and I meant it.

To Isabel.C.Ramsay@gmail.com
From Emer88@iol.ie
Hi, my love. How are you feeling today? The weather is okay, here in Galway.
Emer xxx

To Emer88@iol.ie
From Isabel.C.Ramsay@gmail.com
Please can you speak normally to me again.
I'm not dead.
I'm not eighty-five.
Tell me about your life.
Please?
Isabel x

To Isabel.C.Ramsay@gmail.com
From Emer88@iol.ie
Okay, grand.
*Dear Bell! I've been invited to INDIA. Of all places. Your husband
will eat his heart out, ha! Just joking, it'll be years before I get to his
level. But I'm so excited. I'll be playing with some local musicians.
I want to buy a sari and wear it at my wedding. Which will never
happen because I'm DOOMED when it comes to love. I must
be doomed. There is no other explanation. Last week Ciara tried
to set me up with this ghastly guy who plays the oboe and only
talks about himself. Ciara is obsessed with setting me up and she
always gets it wrong. No wonder, though: ours is a limited pool
– musicians, and the crazy people who are willing to go out with
musicians. Throw in the last variable, me being visually impaired
(like they say on official forms) and you'll get a one-in-a-million
chance of me finding the man of my dreams.*

Anyway. Here, I'm talking rubbish . . . are you still awake?

From Isabel.C.Ramsay@gmail.com
To Emer88@iol.ie
*I am! And it's not rubbish. I love hearing about your life. Clara
is here. She is not bad, actually. The whole thing started quite
strangely. I don't know if I told you this, but I dreamt of her just
before they took me into hospital (don't worry, I won't keep going
on about that, I want to forget all about it too). So anyway I dreamt
of her, and it was a lovely dream. She reminded me of someone, or
maybe it was like I'd known her before. Maybe in a previous life.*

*She's here now, down in the kitchen cooking me a hearty lunch
(this is exactly what she said).*

I sort of like it that she is here.

Weird, I know.

From Emer88@iol.ie

To Isabel.C.Ramsay@gmail.com

Yes, it's pretty weird you dreamt of her, and weird that you enjoy having her there, you big loner, you. No, seriously, I'm so glad you have someone there looking after you. That Morag, she is a human igloo. Anyway. I have to go now, rehearsal with Spiorad. Speak later. I can't wait until you start using the phone again. I miss your voice.

Emer xxx

23

Because nobody knows you like I do

For you
I'll pick all the flowers
In Heaven's meadows

Angus

On the drive back from Glasgow to Glen Avich, the fields and moors were grey and barren. Winter eased itself in slowly at first, and then it fell all of a sudden. I thought of the long, dark days ahead and how they would affect Bell. Near-bare branches lifted their arms to the white sky and whirlpools of the last fallen leaves twirled in front of my car. Our garden would soon be empty, asleep. And Bell loved looking at it from the window. Now she wouldn't have this joy any more.

I wanted to bring some light back into her life, and colours, and a sense of things growing.

Suddenly, an idea came into my mind, and I was so excited my heart started pounding. Listening to the radio, I used the rest of the journey to hatch a plan. Yes, it was perfect. The perfect gift for Bell.

I couldn't wait to bring my plan to fruition, but I needed Margherita's help. I stopped the car in a lay-by and called my brother.

"Torcuil, it's me. Listen, I know you're at the university right now, but I need to get in touch with Margherita."

"Of course, what's up? Where are you, by the way? Sounds windy."

"On my way back to Glen Avich. I'm standing at the side of the road. I just had an idea, for Bell . . . I think Margherita can help. Do you know where I can find her? I'll be home in an hour."

"She'll be in the kitchen at the coffee shop; she has a big job on tomorrow. What idea?"

"It's a surprise. If she has a big job tomorrow maybe I shouldn't bother her today. Maybe I should drop by in a couple of days?"

"I think she'll be happy to help. I'll send you her phone number and you can ask her yourself."

"Great. Thanks!" I waited for a minute for his text to come through.

Can't wait for Friday, to see everyone again. I had such a great time. Bibi xxx

Oh. This wasn't the text I'd been expecting.

She couldn't wait to see *everyone* again? Well, that was nothing controversial.

Then why did I read it as "I can't wait to see *you* again"?

Because I had a vivid imagination, that's all.

I deleted the text quickly. I could not think of an answer.

"Margherita? It's Angus. I'm sorry to bother you on your mobile, is it a good time to talk?"

"Angus, hello! Of course, how can I help you?"

"It's for Isabel. You know the way she doesn't go out much . . ." – or at all, but that seemed so harsh, when it was said aloud – "And also, everything is looking so grey at the moment . . ."

133

"Oh, I know, it's so cold all of a sudden!"

"It is! So I was thinking . . ." I explained my idea in broad paintstrokes. I'd give her the details when we met.

"It sounds great. Come and see me and we can talk about it. I'm at La Piazza."

"Torcuil said you're in the middle of a big job . . ."

"It's not a problem. Honestly, come down and we'll sort it all out."

I stood for a moment in the icy wind, beside my car, looking over the fields, considering Margherita's easy kindness, and feeling, after all, blessed.

"Oh, hello, have you come to steal my cookies?" she said playfully as she saw me. There was something about her that reminded me of sunshine. She stopped for a moment, her hands still in the double oven glove having taken out a tray of biscuits shaped like ponies.

"Absolutely. They smell amazing."

"Thanks! They're for a christening. Now, about your idea. You can go to the outbuildings . . . They shouldn't be locked, but if they are, you know where to look for the key . . ."

"Second drawer on the left in Torcuil's desk?"

"Exactly. I'm so excited for you! It's such a good idea. I wish I'd had it," she said, piping blue icing on some of the pony biscuits she'd made earlier.

"Thank you. That is a great help."

"It's never a bother, you know that." She pronounced "bother" with a Scottish accent, which made me smile, considering she was a London Italian. She'd been here just over a year and already she had a bit of a lilt.

"By the way, I wanted to thank you for something else as

well. You always send Bell cakes and biscuits. It's very kind of you . . . We both really enjoy them . . . Well, it's more than that, really. It's the thought behind it. It's so important for Bell to know she's not forgotten."

"Of course she isn't!" Margherita replied, carefully placing some iced biscuits in transparent bags. "It's no problem, really. I appreciate her little notes when she says she enjoys them. But I'd love nothing more than meeting my sister-in-law for more than a few minutes . . . I'd love to sit down with her for a meal, have a chat, maybe go shopping . . ." she said, and there was a hint of sadness in her eyes.

My stomach churned. I was always afraid that Bell would be blamed for something that wasn't her fault. I was always afraid that even the people closest to us would not understand what she was going through, and how helpless I was. But Margherita didn't blame her and my stomach unknotted when she simply said: "I pray for her every day, you know? And for you."

It was such a kind thing to say. I had no answer.

"Also, she means a lot to Torcuil. I mean, I know about their history. That is also why I'd like to know her better. She's on his mind a lot."

And that was like a small, near-imperceptible stab in my side.

On my way home, my mobile beeped.

Did you have a good time? Bibi xxx

She wouldn't let me get away with not answering, I supposed. I texted quickly as I ran home to see Bell.

Of course

24

The flowers inside (2)

Only you can see
The flowers inside

Isabel

That day, Angus was being a bit strange. First of all, he'd been home two days in a row, which I didn't think could happen when he was so busy with work, and second, he kept sending me upstairs with different excuses. Something was going on.

From my bedroom I heard the front door opening and closing, and then a male voice in the garden. I looked out of the window and saw Dougie's blue van leaving. I was about to get a bit panicky when Angus called me.

"Bell! Can you come down a minute, please?"

I went down the stairs – Angus was at the bottom, with a triumphant expression on his face. "I need to show you something," he said. I followed him through to the living room and into the conservatory.

I was speechless.

The conservatory was overflowing with plants – violets, stephanotis, bulbs growing in water, orchids – and aromatic herbs – rosemary, sage, basil and others I didn't recognise.

It was like a little garden inside the house. The scent was incredible. Lavender, thyme, mint, peonies and even a tiny lilac mixed their scents into the air and made it smell like a summer meadow.

"Of course we'll need to replant the peonies and the lilac at some point . . . Some of the plants will have to be put back outside in the spring, some will need to be changed often, like the basil, Margherita said . . . But you'll always have your indoor garden," Angus said.

"I . . . I can't believe it. This is amazing!" I had tears in my eyes. "Thank you. Oh, thank you, Angus!" I threw my arms around him.

"Well, if Isabel won't go to the garden . . . But remember, this is only temporary. Until you can get outside and enjoy your real garden," Angus said.

My Angus had turned the conservatory into a little piece of heaven. All that was missing was the blue sky and the butterflies.

It was like a dream.

"I wanted you to have some herbs as well. Margherita said you'd love the scent, and also we can use them in the kitchen," Angus said, beaming.

"Margherita helped you?" I said, moved.

"Yes, she and Torcuil gave me all these plants. They thought it was a great idea, to give you a place where you could, you know, breathe, relax."

"It's wonderful. I can't thank you all enough," I said. I was doing my utmost not to cry, but I couldn't help welling up. They'd all been so kind.

"Right. I'll put the kettle on," Angus concluded in perfect Scottish style – when overwhelmed with emotion, either make a cup of tea or have a stiff drink. Left alone in my little indoor garden, I smiled to myself between the tears.

Strange. It must have been a trick of the eye, because I thought I saw a little blue butterfly fluttering among the plants – but then, when I looked again, it was gone.

25

White is for happy

You said to me once
Autumn is our time

Isabel

Everything was bare now, and frozen; winter was here at last. It was a relief. I couldn't wait to leave behind what I'd done that autumn, to forget all about those terrible orange pills. I'd given up on the medicines – trying and failing was just too painful – but not on the hope of recovering by myself. But there were so many blue days that I spent time frozen somewhere in the house or just sleeping the day away.

I found solace in sitting in my indoor garden, in Clara's company. Angus was away a lot, going out early and coming home very, very late, and I missed him. I knew that this was just the beginning, that he would be away with the orchestra even more when he'd take his post properly. Soon it would be time to find a flat in Glasgow and stay over for days on end, not just the odd night crashing at a friend's, like now. The thought of Angus being away frightened me, but with Clara I was never alone. I had thought having Clara there all the time would get on my nerves, considering how used I was to being by myself, but it didn't at all. It was easy. I couldn't believe how close we'd become in such a short period of time. Like I'd known her forever.

We developed a sort of routine, Clara and I. Every time Angus went away for work, she turned up and we'd spend the day together. Whenever Morag came with the groceries, Clara went for a walk and came back with Glen Avich stories.

Like Mairi, who was six years old and had Down's syndrome, landing a place in a theatre company in Aberdeen and appearing on the evening news. Her mum, Pamela, talked about nothing else. Or Inary, Angus's cousin, being shortlisted for a prestigious literary prize and going to collect it in London. Someone starting a tiny library in the community centre, Glen Avich disastrously losing the local shinty championship like every year, a hot-air balloon from the nearby flying club doing an emergency landing in the middle of the play park, an exhibition of spooky pictures made by the local children for Halloween ... Some news was sad, like an accident claiming the life of a young woman and the whole village gathering at the funeral, and some funny, like a Swedish woman, a new resident, applying to hold a witchcraft class in the community centre. Apparently, all the participants had to contribute was a few candles and a ceremonial knife – but that didn't go down very well with the committee. They opted for a Pilates class instead.

Drinking in her stories, it was like being out again, in the middle of life, instead of being holed up here. We sat together, drank tea and chatted. In those moments, I forgot all about the nightmares, the panic. I was just Isabel having a friend for tea, finding out the latest village news.

"Aisling is fit to burst." Clara had told me about Aisling's pregnancy, among the news she brought back from the village. "And she still goes up to La Piazza to lend a hand because

140

Kate is wired to the moon." Clara smiled a mischievous smile.

"And what's the latest about Pablo?" I knew about Kate's boyfriend, who, apparently, had eyelashes as long as a woman's and hips like a salsa dancer – Kate's own words.

"Oh, Pablo just wants to act. His life is the theatre," she said melodramatically. "So although Kate is the love of his life, as he keeps saying in his texts to her, he's not coming up here, he's going to London to study acting. Kate said he's going to be the next Benicio del Toro."

"For sure," I laughed. "But then, can you imagine if he really is successful and we are proved wrong?"

"Then we can say we met him when he was a humble waiter in a tapas bar in Barcelona. Though we didn't really meet him."

"We might soon. I mean . . . you might. I'll be here," I said, and the mood went suddenly dark.

Maybe feeling the change in the atmosphere, Clara changed the subject. "Kate and Aisling bicker a lot, but they seem very close."

"I have a sister too," I added, and I was surprised myself. I didn't usually talk about her. Or my father.

"Do you? Where does she live?"

"She's still in Ireland. Near my dad."

"Are you in touch at all?"

"Not really," I replied, in a tone that said *Don't ask any more*. But Clara wasn't satisfied.

"Why don't you write her a letter?" she asked, and the question hurt like a needle in my eye.

"I don't speak to my sister. I don't speak to my dad either. My dad . . . Well, when my mum died he went a bit crazy. He became obsessed with religion. I think it was his refuge."

141

Clara was silent, waiting for me to continue. And, quite unbelievably, I did. "And there was his new wife too."

Clara's eyes widened slightly. "When did he remarry?"

"I was sixteen."

"And she wasn't good to you?"

"Maura was all right. She and Gillian – my sister – became very close. She tried to get close to me too, but it just didn't work. I mean, she wasn't my mum. I know it sounds terribly childish, but it's true."

I remember very well when she came on the scene. One day, a lady I'd never seen before turned up at the church – Maura. She was tall, with a soft, low voice and a laugh that seemed out of place in the subdued atmosphere of the church. She had long, frizzy hair and the hat she wore sat on top of it like on a soft cushion. She'd never been married and she had no children, our friend Leah told my sister and me. Maura would come to lunch at our house every Sunday after church, and there was something in my father's eyes when he looked at her – something I'd never seen before. Something akin to joy, or at least satisfaction.

I was too young to read the signs – I only realised what was happening when things between her and my dad were pretty much settled.

In preparation for the wedding, Maura took my sister and I on a shopping trip. My sister smiled and chatted a lot, flushed and happy. She was now nearly twenty-three and she loved being involved in our father's wedding. There was a strange aura of triumph around her, almost a sense of vengeance. I knew it was about punishing my mum. She'd left us, and now finally my dad was finding happiness – with another woman.

Gillian and I were trying on bridesmaid dresses: the deep

plum colour Maura had chosen made Gillian's black hair and white skin stand out even more, and made me look washed out. Or so I thought. Maura didn't seem to look at it that way – she looked at me with shining eyes and raised a hand to stroke my face, but I turned away. To this day, I regret that gesture – because she never tried again.

The day after the wedding, I left home.

But there was no point in telling Clara all that. She nodded, both hands cupping her mug of tea, her head down.

"As I was growing up I always felt like . . ."

"Like what?" Clara said softly.

"Like I was walking on thin ice. All the time. That any moment I could fall through. And then I did." I shrugged.

"I'm sorry," she murmured.

"It's not your fault. And anyway, I'll get better. I'm sure I will. One day."

"You will. You're taking your medicines, and they'll help." A knot of guilt in my stomach, because I wasn't taking my medicines at all.

"You know, I knew someone . . . a friend of mine. She was unwell for years, but then, when she was pregnant with her second daughter, it got worse. There was no help at the time, you know . . . The doctor just told her to rest, to eat. Her husband didn't really understand, so she confided in me. We drove to the nearest town, to a Chinese doctor. He gave her some herbal pills. He said take white for happy, green for baby! He was very nice. And he predicted she was going to have a little girl."

"And did the pills work?"

"Not the Chinese ones, no. She was unlucky. Nowadays there is so much help available; doctors and medicines can help so much. But then her baby girl was born . . ."

143

"What was her name?"

A hesitation. "Sonia. She loved Russian names, you see. We both loved Russian culture—"

"So did my mum!"

Clara smiled. "Really?"

"She had a collection of matryoshkas, you know, the little Russian dolls . . . I don't know what happened to the dolls. So tell me more about your friend. What happened after Sonia was born?"

"She got better. A lot better. And she was happy again," Clara concluded.

"That's great," I replied, and a sense of relief streaked through me, leaving me light, weightless. It seemed like a good omen, that this unknown woman had recovered on her own. Maybe I would too.

At that moment, Clara's phone beeped.

"Well, the latest news is that Kate is actually engaged!"

"She *is*? You told me she's sixteen . . ."

"Yes, but apparently she says that in the Twilight books Bella Swan marries and has a baby at seventeen."

"Oh, well then! If Bella Swan did it . . ." I laughed.

It was strange how Clara managed to make me laugh even in the middle of a sad conversation.

"So, Pablo. We'll meet him together, when he comes up. At la Piazza. Margherita will make paella and we'll dance the flamenco for him."

All of a sudden, as she spoke those words, my mood changed again. I would not be at La Piazza. I'd be stuck at home. I couldn't forget that although I was feeling a little better, I was still living in a prison.

Some spark of the old me ignited in my chest, a stubborn

144

little flame that refused to be extinguished. "I'll show you my studio, if you like." I couldn't believe I was saying those words.

"I would love to see it," she said simply. Like it wasn't that huge a deal. She was being cautious, treating me like I was a horse she didn't want to bolt.

She followed me upstairs and then up the metal spiral staircase that led to my studio. I took the steps one at a time, slowly, and opened the door like I was opening the room in the story of Bluebeard. The scent of colours hit my nostrils and I breathed in, breathed *deeply*. And then I couldn't wait to be inside, so I went in quickly and closed my eyes for a moment as I inhaled more of the beautiful, familiar scent. The scent of my work. When I opened my eyes again, the golden light of dawn had filled the room all of a sudden, in one of those moments that are like unexpected gifts that you can slip among your memories and keep there.

"The view from up here is incredible," Clara said, gazing out of the small window at the opposite side of the room.

And it was. I stepped slowly across the floor and looked over to the loch. The dawn was like liquid gold and it spilled on our faces. Suddenly, she spotted the sleeping bag folded in two on a chair.

"Do you use this as a guest room?" she asked.

"No, I used to sleep in here sometimes. When Angus was away for work. I liked being among my work and I liked the smell of paint."

She smiled. "I can imagine. It must be wonderful, to have such a talent. Such a passion."

I didn't say anything. I didn't say I felt like I was losing it all.

All of a sudden, I wanted to go. I just wanted to be out of my studio and downstairs, cleaning or watching some stupid

TV show. It seemed a dead space without me working in it.

"This is beautiful. If I were you, I'd spend my days here," she continued, but when she saw my face she probably wondered if she'd said the wrong thing. The golden light, the rays of dawn vanished and grey ones replaced them.

"I don't know if I'll ever be able to work again," I whispered.

"You will."

"How do you know? You don't know me, Clara," I said a bit harshly. "You've seen my studio now," I said, and began to make my way down.

26

The scent of colours (2)

The gift inside
It calls me

Isabel

That night, after having spent the day with Clara, I tossed and turned. The whole day had been so weird. Having a stranger in the house . . . who didn't feel like a stranger. Telling her about my father and Gillian. And most of all, I couldn't believe I'd been up to my studio.

Yes, that was the most surreal event. After months of trying, after all the tears I'd cried because my studio felt like such a dead place and I didn't want to set foot in it . . . I'd finally gone up.

And it felt like I'd brought something back with me; it felt like I had brought *the scent of colours* with me. I kept smelling paint on my skin, in my hair. And an image played before my eyes – a blue butterfly in a lush, colourful garden . . .

I was restless. Angus was sleeping soundly, exhausted after the long drive back. I sat up and slipped off the bed.

"What's wrong?" came Angus's sleepy voice.

"I have an idea for a picture."

"But it's the middle of the night . . ."

"I know. You sleep, okay?" I whispered, tucking the duvet

around him and running my hand through his hair, as if he were a sleeping child. I stood up and quickly pulled my jeans on and slipped a cardigan over my nightie. The night was very still and silent, and I was frightened. But not frightened of the dark.

Frightened of not feeling the spark again.

Would I be able to work, I asked myself as I tiptoed up the spiral staircase? Or would it be a complete failure? I was panting in fear, my heart racing, and still I couldn't let myself go back to bed. It was the scent of colours that called me.

I walked into the attic and pressed the light switch.

It was so peaceful.

A time that was mine alone.

Slowly, I sat at my working table. Everything was still like I'd left it the day I realised I couldn't work any more. An illustration from the *Scottish Legends* book – an enchanted piper in a cave made of gold overcoming a dragon with his music – sat unfinished. But something made me put that drawing aside and find a fresh piece of paper. I switched the desk light on.

And my fingers hovered over the colours: the pencils, the watercolours, the oil paints. I could hear myself breathing, the fast breath of a little bird caught somewhere.

I was so afraid to open that part of me again, but I couldn't stop.

I choose a pencil: deep, deep blue.

And oh, it felt good as it glided on the paper, the colour soft, malleable. Spreading like butter. I drew like I was possessed, and when I was finished, the paper was full of blue butterflies dancing in a tropical garden.

27

Butterfly

This chrysalis I see
I watch her wait

Isabel

"Bell! Oh my God, Bell!"

Angus's cries resounded all over the house, and I awoke with a jolt. For a moment I didn't know where I was, then I remembered: I had started to doze at my table and then, half-asleep, had cocooned myself in the sleeping bag on the floor of my studio. I blinked, my eyes sticky with tiredness. I rubbed my left eye, only to realise that my fingers had paint on them. Just like old times.

"I'm here! I'm okay!" I called, and dragged myself up, slightly dizzy.

"Bell!" came his panicked call again.

"Angus! I'm here! In my studio!"

"Bell!" I heard his footsteps, and I hurried down the spiral staircase.

"I'm sorry. I didn't think . . ." I said as I made my way down as quickly as I could without falling. He was standing on the landing looking up, as pale as a ghost.

"Thank God. I woke up and the bed was empty, I couldn't find you . . ."

"I'm sorry," I repeated. He held me tight, kisses on my hair, on my face.

"I thought I'd lost you."

I think that was the first time I realised how scared he really was for me. I wrapped my arms around him and kissed his cheeks, and then his mouth, over and over again.

"I'm okay. Really."

"What were you doing? You're hurt . . . Your eye . . ."

"That's just paint," I said, letting him rub it off my eye. "I was working. And then I fell asleep up there, you know I keep a sleeping bag in case—"

"You were *working*?" he said.

"Yes. I was illustrating a story. About butterflies in a magical garden."

"But this is amazing . . . Bell, you haven't worked for *months*."

"I know. This . . . Well, it just came out."

Angus held me tight again. "It's okay. You are okay," he whispered into my hair.

"I kept smelling the colours on me."

"Will you show me?"

I smiled and said nothing, I just took his hand and led him upstairs, to my studio. My work table was, as usual, very tidy even in the middle of work – I had to keep things organised and nice to look at; it was my nature. The watercolours and oil paints – I was using both – were neatly arranged – and several glasses of coloured water were lined at the edge of the table. All around the desk were shelves, put up for me by Angus, filled to the brim with art materials and different kinds of paper. There was a corkboard hanging beside me, full of postcards and sketches, and on the other side a small bookshelf with all my art books. It was my favourite corner of the house. The best thing was that it looked alive again – not abandoned.

"Is this it? Bell, it's beautiful!" Angus said, lightly touching the edge of my work in progress. In the colourful garden, among the butterflies, ran a little girl in a summer dress. In the foreground, close up, I had drawn a chrysalis, waiting to open and reveal its magical content to the world.

"Do you really think so?" I wasn't fishing for compliments; I'd always been insecure, now, after so many months of inactivity, more than ever.

"Yes. I think it's one of your best pieces yet. It's . . . inspired. Is it a stand-alone?"

"I don't think so. I'd like it to be a story . . . a picture book. Not necessarily for children, though."

"I'm so proud of you," he said. That was the best compliment I could ever hope for.

Dancing with butterflies

And I'd walk and walk and walk
I'd walk barefoot and drained
All the way to where the land meets the water
Of my creation

Isabel

I'd never showed my work in progress to anyone but Angus, but it felt natural to show Clara. I was a bit apprehensive as she gazed at my picture in silence. Maybe she wouldn't like it. Maybe my work wasn't as good as it used to be before I got ill, but Angus hadn't wanted to say in order not to hurt my feelings. I knew I would only get an objective opinion when I sent it to my agent, and I had no plans, then, to do so – but my heart was in my throat anyway.

"It came into my mind because I keep seeing blue butterflies," I explained nervously. "And you never see butterflies in winter. It's inspired by the garden Angus made for me, but made magical . . . like it's out of a dream."

"Isabel, it's amazing," she said finally. "You have such talent!" she added, with one of those serene smiles of hers. I felt myself blushing, and for a moment I was a bit choked. I felt so lucky – when I had no faith in myself, both my husband and Clara believed in me. "Can't you see?" she said. "Can't you see how beautiful your work is?"

"Thank you. I'm thinking of turning it into a story. A picture book. It's called *Chrysalis* . . . and it's about a butterfly. As you probably guessed!" I laughed.

I felt happy. Maybe just for a moment, but I felt happy.

That seemed like a miracle in itself.

I remembered something Angus had said to me years ago, after he'd finished working on a composition that had left him exhausted and glowing: "Happiness comes from creation."

He was right.

And I had always, always known it.

I spent the day in my studio and didn't even come downstairs for lunch. Clara brought me a baked potato and tea at some point, but I didn't stop for more than twenty minutes. The story was sweeping me away, just like my work used to, and it felt amazing. It felt *right*.

Every once in a while, as I gazed out of the small window, I realised once again how lovely the view from my studio was – how beautiful my loch was.

After dinner, I went back to the studio. Clara was due to sleep in my house, because Angus was away in Glasgow and would stay away until tomorrow. After working for about an hour, I heard Clara's voice calling me from downstairs.

"It's best if you don't get too tired, Isabel," she said.

It was strange to be looked after this way. I don't think I ever had been, not even when I was a little girl. I had never experienced something like this, not until I met Angus, and even then it was different.

Maybe this was what having a mother felt like.

I kneeled close to the stairs and called out, "I know, sorry. I'll go to bed now."

"Well, if you can't sleep, you can come and share some warm milk and cookies with me."

"Yes please!" I said, and put my work to sleep for the night.

"You're never too old for milk and cookies." Clara smiled as she placed a plate in front of me. I hadn't eaten so much in months. And I was even allowing someone else to cook in my kitchen.

We sat in quiet companionship – it was so peaceful. And still, a thought kept stinging me. I was still not taking my medication.

I had tried twice more, but I just couldn't. In my mind, it was like drinking poison. And I knew that even if I had returned to work, even if I was feeling better, those medicines had been prescribed for a reason. Because I needed them.

It was a battle, and the battleground was my mind. And for now, I was losing.

"Isabel."

"Yes?"

"What time do you take your pills? Because I never see you—"

"Well, I haven't yet. I'd said to Angus I would start on Monday."

"When did you say that to him?" she asked gently.

"The day they let me out of the hospital."

"That was weeks ago, Isabel."

"Oh . . . I must have forgotten," I said with a reassuring smile. "I'll take them tomorrow morning."

"Would you like me to remind you? If you show me what you have to take—"

"No, thanks, it's okay. I'll do it myself. I'm tired now," I said and stood up. "Goodnight, Clara."

Her eyes studied my face. "Goodnight, Isabel."

The next morning I got up when it was still dark, so that I could try to take my meds before Clara woke up. There was no way I could tell them my secret, Clara or Angus. There was no way I could explain to them I couldn't take my medication and ask for help, though I was desperate for someone to help me overcome this. A part of me, the lucid part of me, the one that whispered among the screams of my panic, knew that I had to take my medication and was desperate for help, that taking it could really improve things for me. Make me better. Maybe even make me recover.

I lined up the bottle and the blister pack. I prepared a glass with water in it.

But I couldn't get past the idea they were poison – my panic screamed too loud for my rational mind to be heard. Drying my tears, I replaced the cap and threw out the pill. I knew it was going to be a bad day. A blue day, I called it in my mind.

Defeated, I just sat and cried and cried, until Clara came to find me.

"What's wrong?" she said, alarm painted all over her face.

"Nothing. Just a moment. Just a moment."

"Are you okay? You got too tired yesterday. I knew you shouldn't have worked so hard. Have you taken your medicine?" she said, gazing at the bottle and the little box.

"Yes. It's fine. It's all fine."

She just gazed at me, uncertain as to what to say next – I could read it in her face.

"I'm just going to sit here for a bit, Clara, if that's okay. You just . . . do your thing . . ."

"Of course. I have some laundry to fold; I can do it here and keep you company."

"Oh, please, you're not here to do the housework," I protested.

"It's no trouble. Maybe you could come upstairs with me and we could put the clothes away."

I shook my head. "No. I'm just going to sit here for a while." I knew there would be no work today.

I had this thing: if I was immobile, if I moved as little as possible – barely enough to go to the bathroom or grab a glass of water – the universe wouldn't notice I existed and it would not send some terrible catastrophe to me. So I did that. Even when Clara tried to get me to do things and stand up, I sat at the table like a limpet clinging to its rock, refusing to move.

I know. Weird. But it was one of those rituals that kept me going and helped me deal with panic when it struck. Sometimes I sat at the kitchen table, sometimes in the living room, hugging my knees on the sofa and watching day turn into night. Sometimes I curled up in the bedroom, gazing at the loch – looking at it for hours on end, without moving.

Thinking of my mum.

Clara went about her business without bothering me; I preferred it that way, and I was grateful. She made me lunch – I had explained that a cheese and ham toastie and a hot chocolate was what would get me through a blue day, no other food would do – and occasionally she touched my shoulder, and I was so grateful for that contact, in the painful rigidity of my panic, I could have cried. Finally, the sun set and it was dark. Thank God, the blue day was ending. Angus came back and it was time for Clara to go. I heard them whispering in the hall.

I tried to forget I was deceiving them both by not taking my medicines.

I tried to forget that I was deceiving the love of my life.

I don't know what to do, I thought in dismay and felt the tears swell in my eyes once more – no, he couldn't find me crying.

"Hey, baby . . . Clara said you had a bad day . . ."

"No, no. I'm fine. Just . . ." I wracked my mind for an excuse and I couldn't find one. "Just one of those days. Blue. I'm sorry."

He held me in his arms and I just stayed there, in the comfort of his woollen checked shirt, breathing in the scent of Angus, the scent of comfort and home.

"Don't apologise, my love," he said, and rocked me gently, like you would rock a child who's had a nightmare. "You even worked again, didn't you? Remember, your butterflies . . ."

I sighed imperceptibly, thinking of how much I would have loved to spend the day in my studio, instead of immobile and frozen at the table, desperately trying to *disappear*.

"You've been taking your meds for weeks now, so soon we'll see some improvement, the doctor said, remember?"

Six weeks, and the medicines should work. Yes, the doctor had said that. But for that to happen, I had to take them.

If only I could force myself to down them, I thought, burying my face deeper into his chest. If only I could dissolve this idiotic belief that the pills would kill me like they'd killed my mother, or so my dad said. But Dad's voice still resounded in my ears and I couldn't silence it.

I waited until Angus was upstairs getting changed, and then I stood up.

One last try.

One last try.

Again, I poured the drops; again, I took a pill out of the blister pack.

My hands shook so much I could barely hold the glass . . .

And then I poured all my drops down the sink, tears streaming down my face.

Poison

Like climbing
A smooth wall
Like drinking
A butterfly's tears

Isabel

I tried again to take my medicines. Twice. And again they ended up down the sink. But I was telling everyone I was taking them, and the deception was killing me inside.

My father's voice was stronger than ever.

Sometimes I think of those terrible stories of children being hit, abused, and my heart goes out to them: my father never laid a hand on me, and still he damaged me more deeply than I can ever say.

"So, what's the plan for this morning?" Clara asked softly, shaking me out of my thoughts. Once again I was sitting at the kitchen table, my medication laid out in front of me. I jumped at the sound of her voice.

"What's wrong?"

"Nothing. I'm fine. I'm okay. Just a bit . . ."

I put all the medicines away. The liquid in the little bottle was going down steadily, and the blister pack was nearly empty – it was time to get some more – but none of it was ending up in my body.

"I think I'm going to do some work on *Chrysalis*," I said. I didn't meet Clara's eyes as I hurried upstairs into my studio.

I knew Clara could sense that something was off, but she couldn't tell what – yet. Something told me that she would soon begin to suspect I wasn't taking my medicines, if she didn't already.

30

Life in a fishbowl

Within you I found
Peace

Torcuil

It was a Saturday morning, and Leo and I had dropped in to La Piazza to visit Margherita, who was working. Lara was, as she often was now, hanging out with her new friends from school. Lara had felt isolated and misunderstood in her school in London, so when she'd moved up here it had been a relief for her and her mother that she got on so well with the local kids. She also often spent time with my cousin, Inary, with whom she shared a passion for writing.

Things had changed for me too in the past year – life had turned upside down with Margherita's arrival, in a way I couldn't have imagined. For the better, in every way. In the past, on a Saturday morning I wouldn't have been just sitting and chatting – I would have been rushing about with a long to-do list. I was on a hamster's wheel, but, looking back, it was me who couldn't stop. Now I was even busier with my work and the riding school, and Ramsay Hall was now open to the public, not to mention living with a four-year-old whom I loved dearly – but everything was *calmer*. I could just sit and watch the flames in my fireplace, in silence, because Margherita was at my side and grey thoughts and sad memories were kept at bay. Yes, she had changed my life.

"You okay?" she asked me suddenly.

"Yes, why?"

"You were staring at me."

'Sorry," I said, and looked into my coffee cup. I wasn't about to start gushing in front of Debora. But Margherita must have read my thoughts, because she smiled. And then, her face became serious again.

"Did he call this morning?" I knew who she meant. Angus and I had spoken nearly every day, since Izzy . . . since she'd done what she did.

"No . . ."

Kate, Aisling's sister, cut in. "He hasn't called for two days now! I'm in bits."

I was dumbfounded. "Sorry?"

"Kate, Margherita wasn't talking about Pablo," Debora explained patiently.

"Oh, I thought you'd want to know if he'd called. Well, I'll let you know all the same."

I stifled a laugh. "So how are things with you two, Kate?"

"We broke up. Last time we broke up we were back together by the evening, so now I'm worried," she said, looking at the phone she carried in the pocket of her apron. "It's when you know he's the one . . . When you know he's your destiny . . . that's when things become complicated. You have to treat your love like a precious flower," she said solemnly, and this time I couldn't help laughing openly.

"Kate. You are sixteen," Margherita said.

"Juliet was a teenager when she fell for Romeo," she replied.

"Juliet ended up dead in a crypt. Now clear those tables,

Kate," Debora called from the counter, a twinkle in her eye.

"Anyway," I continued. "No, we didn't speak this morning. I'll phone him later."

"Okay, let me know what he says, if there's any news. I need to go back to work, I'm up to my eyes here! I'm catering for a wedding and my filo-pastry brie tartlets just burnt to a crisp," she said. She looked unfazed, though. Margherita seemed to be always chilled, whatever the circumstances. "Come with me to the kitchen."

A sudden thought came into my mind. "I was hoping you'd write a recipe for me," I said, following her through the back.

"Sure," she said, taking a sweet-scented tray of meringues out of the oven. "Anything in particular?"

"Apple and cinnamon cake. Isabel loves it when you send it . . . I was thinking maybe she and Clara could make it. But don't worry if you're too busy."

"Not at all," she said kindly, and grabbed a pad with a shopping list and some notes on it. She scribbled the recipe on a fresh page, tore it off and gave it to me. "For her eyes only. Burn after reading. It's a secret recipe."

"Is it really?"

"Of course not! Let me know how she gets on."

"Thanks. I'm off then. I'll phone Angus and give you a ring if there's any news."

"Of Pablo, you mean?" she said, and giggled the way she does, like there is so much to laugh and smile about in this world.

Margherita had the sun in her heart.

I went to Peggy's shop with Leo and bought the ingredients listed in the recipe, but she didn't have any apples, so I walked

163

back to Ramsay Hall and drove to Kinnear. There I bought some apples and then, at the post office, a cardboard box and some twine. I put all the ingredients and the recipe in the box, tied it with the twine and left it in front of Debora's house, so Clara would find it, with a little note: *For Isabel and Clara*.

Like opening a little umbrella in the middle of a typhoon.

But it was something. It was all I could do, these little things that lay between being looked after and being forgotten.

31

Cinnamon

The times when I try
To change the past
The times when I try
To lead you home

Isabel

Once again, Angus was away in Glasgow. I remember at our wedding a friend of his, Margaret, joked that you should never marry a musician – you'd end up being a sort of widow, losing your husband to music. It was a bit late to warn me, considering I had just pronounced my vows and was standing in front of her in my white, lacy dress, a bouquet of yellow roses in my hands, tipsy with champagne and happiness.

I was unafraid, then – there would never be a time when I resented his work, his passion, because he'd never resent mine.

I would have never thought, back then, when I was strong and independent, that I would feel so lost whenever he went.

But that cold, cold morning, I only had a moment to be sad as he pulled away from the driveway, because Clara arrived with a big smile and a cardboard box, her silver earrings swinging as she walked, a bright-red scarf around her neck.

"Look what I've got!"

"Oh, what is it?"

"Come and see," she said, placing the box on the kitchen table.

"Oh, it's food . . . There's a note!"

Clara read it out to me: "*All you need to make apple and cinnamon cake.*"

"There are all the ingredients . . . Look . . . Apples, flour, eggs . . . She even put in a little bag of cinnamon sticks with a tiny grater!" A little spark of joy ignited in me. "Okay. I'm not the best at cooking, but I swear I'm going to do my best," I said. "What about you?"

"Not a clue about baking either . . . but we'll make it."

"My mum was the same," I said, and there was a little silence.

"What do you mean?"

"She hated cooking, or so I was told." I shrugged. Talking about her was hard, and at the same time so sweet. "My sister said that once she gave us hot chocolate and marshmallows for dinner. My dad was furious – he was all for stodge, you know, a roast dinner and that kind of thing. But I think it must have been so much fun. If only I could remember . . ."

Clara was quiet for a little while.

We spent a wonderful hour, laughing and cooking together. It was one of those moments when, miraculously, I forgot all about my predicament and I was just . . . myself. It happened very rarely, that I could forget what was going on in my head and stop listening to the constant panicked inner dialogue. When it did, it was like a precious gift.

I thought of Margherita and how thoughtful she'd been.

"Margherita always has these little gifts for me," I said thoughtfully. "I'd like to paint a picture for her."

"That's a lovely idea. But it wasn't her, this time. Debora told me it was Torcuil."

Torcuil.

166

It was my turn to be quiet, now. And then, as I switched one of the gas rings on to melt some sugar for the caramel topping, the flame fizzled and danced so high it nearly burnt my fingers.

"Ouch!"

"Are you okay?"

"Yes, I'm fine."

"We need to ask Dougie to fix this ring," she said. "It burns all wonky."

"Maybe it just needs cleaning," I replied hopefully.

The idea of having someone other than Angus or Clara in the house horrified me. I would put it off as long as I could.

We just worked together and I wanted nothing to break the spell . . . but just as I was putting the cake in the oven, Clara's phone rang.

"It's Debora," she mouthed. "Yes? Oh, that's wonderful news! And how is she? Great. Thanks for letting us know. That's absolutely wonderful. I can't wait to see them. Yes. Bye!"

She pressed the red button. She was beaming. "Aisling had a baby boy. They called him Eoin."

"Oh, congratulations . . ." I said. To my surprise, my mood had clouded over all of a sudden. I forced a smile. "That's wonderful! Babies are not for me, though," I said, trying to sound flippant.

"But why? Having a child is wonderful, Isabel, and it's all ahead of you!" she said, and I had to stop myself from rolling my eyes. It was such a cliché. Having a baby was wonderful – for other people. And it certainly wasn't a remedy for all ills.

I closed the oven door, maybe a bit too forcefully.

"No, you don't understand. I can't *possibly* have a baby."

"There is no reason why you can't—"

"Because then I'll leave it, like my mum did." I shrugged, and the cruelty of those words, and the truth of them, cut deep.

"I think you'd make a wonderful mum, Isabel. And however you feel about your mum, it doesn't mean you'll be the same," she said gently.

"My mum was wonderful." I defended her. I couldn't help it. "Too wonderful for this world," I said, and all the sadness in the universe was weighing on my heart.

"That looks good," Clara said calmly, gesturing to the cake baking in the oven. "Angus will love it. If there's any left by the time he comes home!"

That was Clara. When sadness threatened to overcome me, she didn't fall into the hole with me – she offered me a hand to climb out of it.

"Maybe we can send a few slices to Margherita. So she can see what we've made out of her parcel," I said.

"That's a lovely idea. I bet it's as good as the ones she makes."

"We can make it again. We can try new recipes . . ."

"Yes. I'd love that," she said, and the darkness, somehow, seemed to have been diffused once again. Strange, how Clara seemed to have that effect on me – like a candle in the darkest of nights.

32

All about your colours

Under a foreign sky
I think of you

From Emer88@iol.ie
To Isabel.C.Ramsay@gmail.com
I'm back. It was just five days but very eventful. India is incredible; you have to go. Anyway, straight to the point. I met someone.

And he came back with me to Ireland!

This is how it happened. I was coming down from the stage, holding Donal's hand as usual, when I tripped! Poor Fatina tried but there was nothing she could do: she even yelped – you know the way she never barks, she is such a quiet dog – but she got a fright, and so did I. But someone was there to get me! And so we ended up going to dinner and then to his hotel room, but we didn't do anything. I mean, we just kissed. He's French. It looks like maybe I won't need Plan B – you know, the way Donal and I decided that if we are both single by the time we are thirty, we get married. Michel plays the piano, thank God, because when I was going out with Innes I swear I thought my ears would fall off! Remember those bagpipes? Lord Almighty, losing my hearing as well as my sight, now that would be fun. But the most exciting thing of all: there were lots of musicians there from all over the world, and they all went back to their own countries, but not Michel. He changed the tickets and came to Ireland! He is staying with me now. It's all very passionate and romantic. Donal says it won't last, but he is always so pessimistic when it comes to my boyfriends.

And you? What have you been doing while I was away?

Yours,

In love,

Emer

And me? What have I been doing? Pretending to take my medication and instead pouring it down the sink, sitting at the window too zonked out to do anything, reading the same stupid books over and over again to stave off anxiety.

I was in quicksand, to sum it up. Sinking slowly. I concocted a quick reply that didn't give away the extent of my distress, but didn't send it and switched the computer off. I pondered other people's lives. I pondered if mine was always going to be this way.

But wait. I had some good news, after all. I'd started painting again. That was worth telling.

From Isabel.C.Ramsay@gmail.com

To Emer88@iol.ie

Well, I'm still stuck in the house. But I started painting again. It feels all weird, I'm so rusty, but it's progress. I don't know how I ever stopped. I missed it so much.

Bell x

From Emer88@iol.ie

To Isabel.C.Ramsay@gmail.com

Oh, Bell, that's the best news ever! No wonder you missed it! I

don't know what I'd do if I couldn't sing and play. I would be lost.
I'm so delighted! What are you working on?

From Isabel.C.Ramsay@gmail.com
To Emer88@iol.ie
I'm supposed to work on some illustrations for a book on Scottish
Legends. But I'm doing something myself. It's a story called
Chrysalis. *Remember I told you Angus made a sort of indoor*
garden for me? Well, it's about a little blue butterfly ... But it's not
finished yet.

From Emer88@iol.ie
To Isabel.C.Ramsay@gmail.com
Oh, I can't wait for you to tell me more about it. I wish I could see
what you do. I mean, you can hear my music, but I can't see your
work ... but you can tell me about it, can't you? I can just picture
you in your studio again. It smelled of wood and paint and you
were so happy there. I don't know how to ask this, Isabel, but ...
does this mean you're making progress?

From Isabel.C.Ramsay@gmail.com
To Emer88@iol.ie
I don't know, to be honest with you. I still can't contemplate going
out. I'm still scared all the time. But I'm painting. I don't think I
can ask for more, at the moment.
  No, that's a lie. I want more. I want to get out of this house and
have a normal life.

From Emer88@iol.ie
To Isabel.C.Ramsay@gmail.com
You'll be fine again; you'll be yourself again.

I believe in you.

And then I can come and see you or you can come and see me and you can tell me all about your colours.

Emer xxx

From BGiffordblue@gmail.com

To AngusRamsay@gmail.com

Hi Angus! Just to say, I can't wait for our gig in Manchester. Spend a bit of time together, catch up ... Today it was so frantic! Everybody says you're doing great. I think you're going places, Angus. You have so much talent: I'm in awe of what you do. And how is Isabel?

See you soon,

Bibi x

From AngusRamsay@gmail.com

To BGiffordblue@gmail.com

Hi Bibi, I'm looking forward to Manchester too. Yes, Bell is still a bit under the weather but she'll be fine very soon.

Angus

33

When I'm not with you

In the shell of a laughter
A world of sunshine and life

Angus

"And here's the CD I was telling you about. I loved it."

"Oh, great. It'll fill the nights I'm away from home. Thank you."

We were in Manchester, on a break from rehearsal. Kyoko and Malcolm, who were on trial with me, were chatting with the conductor, and Bibi and I were left alone. Again.

She was wearing a woollen dress the colour of mist, and her hair was tied back. But why would I notice what she was wearing? I don't even notice what *I'm* wearing.

"It must be hard, to have a family and leave it behind."

"It is, I suppose. But Bell understands. She's used to it."

"She must miss you."

"She does, yes, and I miss her. But I couldn't do anything else."

"I know what you mean. I'm the same. I could never stop playing, never."

"Do you have a family back in Tennessee?"

"My mom and a little brother. I also had a boyfriend, but hey, with the ocean between us . . . it ended."

"Right."

"I saw someone else for a while, another musician. He was more understanding, but we kept missing each other, I was always travelling, he was always travelling and . . . Well, it fizzled out. We're good friends."

"I see."

"When you're on the road so often, you tend to lean on the people around you. It's just the way it works."

I say nothing.

"Maybe we could try to get away for dinner tonight."

"I . . . I think I'm going to have an early night. Thanks anyway."

She looked down with a smile, but I could see her disappointment.

34

Other people's lives

Late-night pictures
Of other people's lives
Reflected like a stranger in a shop window

Isabel

Angus was home, at last, after a few days away. I was so happy to finally spend some time with him.

He was in the shower when his phone beeped. There was a message. Before I knew it, I picked it up, then I put it down again. I'd never been jealous before, never – the thought of it used to make me cringe, like something pathetic, ridiculous. Checking his phone, checking his pockets. That was something only paranoid women did, certainly not me. I was sure of his love. There was no fear in my heart at all, and just as well, because with his job he was bound to meet many other girls, and a lot of them would find him fascinating. People on a stage always seem to have a halo, some sort of mystique, maybe a kind of musical spell. It had certainly worked on me. But I was never worried. The bond Angus and I had was so deep, I couldn't imagine that anyone would be able to break it. Jealousy just didn't seem necessary.

Until now.

My illness had made me far removed, had taken me away from the ones I love, including Angus.

So I looked at the phone, and it said:

It was lovely seeing you, Bibi x

A kiss.

Well, a kiss means nothing, I thought. Friends send each other kisses all the time in emails and texts. But he had never mentioned this girl. And anyway, what kind of name was *Bibi*?

I googled her name, hating myself for it. I know, I know, pathetic. And I regretted it the moment her website came up, full of lovely pictures of her and her gigs, and listings of all the wonderful things she did, her travels, the accounts of her adventures. While I was stuck in my house, frozen at the kitchen table and pouring medicines down the sink, or sleeping my days away, she lived. Bibi's passion for music shone through every picture, every word on her website – and it was a passion she could share with my husband. My non-existent musical talent had always been an inside joke between us, something endearing, and it had never seemed a problem to me. Just the opposite, actually. Angus always said he preferred to be with someone who didn't work in music. He said he was like a balloon with his music, floating in the sky, always on the verge of running away forever – but I held on to him, so he could never get lost. He said I was *serene*, and this serenity kept him grounded.

So much for serene, I thought as I pressed play on a YouTube video, watching Bibi's beautiful, animated face as she played. *Why am I doing this to myself?* It was just torture.

And anyway, there was nothing I could do to prevent *it* from happening, if it had to happen. I could not stop my husband looking for life somewhere else, when all he got from me was despair. I couldn't do anything: except get better, get my life back, share happiness with Angus instead of just misery. Find again all the things we used to do, simple things like sharing a bottle of wine in front of the fire and chatting about our day. Listening to him playing, showing him my work. Walking slowly around the loch, going for coffee, or just *being*. Being that girl he'd fallen for again, being serene again.

If only I knew how to do that.

To Emer88@iol.ie
From Isabel.C.Ramsay@gmail.com
Do you think I should take up the fiddle?

To Isabel.C.Ramsay@gmail.com
From Emer88@iol.ie
No, I think you should stick to the paints. One musician per family is enough anyway. Why are you asking?

To Emer88@iol.ie
From Isabel.C.Ramsay@gmail.com
Nothing . . . just . . . I don't know. Angus has a colleague who's very pretty and very talented. And who manages to get out of the house, which is more than can be said about me.

To Isabel.C.Ramsay@gmail.com
From Emer88@iol.ie
Angus only has eyes for you, my dear. Honestly, don't worry about him. He loves you so much that no pretty colleague will ever turn his head. By the way, are you talking about Bibi Gifford?

The fact that Emer had heard of her alarmed me even more. My heart was pounding as I replied.

To Emer88@iol.ie
From Isabel.C.Ramsay@gmail.com
How did you know?

To Isabel.C.Ramsay@gmail.com
From Emer88@iol.ie
Well, my friend who works with the RSNO saw her a while ago in a coffee shop, and Angus was there, or so she told me, but I didn't think of telling you because I thought nothing of it. Oh God, I've made things worse now, haven't I? But honestly, Angus only has eyes for you. And you know that. So forget this whole conversation because it means nothing!

To Emer88@iol.ie
From Isabel.C.Ramsay@gmail.com
Of course. Don't worry. Signing off now x

That night I couldn't sleep. Maybe Angus still only had eyes for me. But imagine, just imagine how his life could be if he wasn't burdened with me. If he had someone like Bibi by his side. From the pictures, from the tone of her writing, she seemed breezy, happy, full of life. She seemed all that I used to be, or at least a part of me – a part I had lost.

For a moment, I wondered if I should ask Angus about Bibi. And then I rejected the thought. I'd never been jealous before. Angus would only take offence, if I didn't trust him.

Also, I didn't want to know.

If you don't want to hear the answer, don't ask the question.

35

Deception

If I could swap these walls
For the sky above

Isabel

I had forgotten to "take" my medicines. Clara and Angus checked them regularly, so every day I poured a bit in the sink and threw a pill away.

Angus had been away for a few days now and was due back that night; I was counting the hours. Clara was upstairs folding some laundry. The coast seemed clear, so I took the blister pack and the bottle out as quickly as I could. As usual, seeing the medicines lined up, salvation so close and so out of reach, brought tears to my eyes. The litany of guilt began again. If only I could find the strength in myself to forget my father's voice . . . If only I could allow myself to start therapy, to give myself a chance . . .

Helpless tears rolled down my cheeks as I opened the bin and threw my daily pill inside, and then began to drip drip drip the medicine down the sink. Just as I was doing that, I heard my name being called. Clara was coming. I hadn't heard her footsteps in the hall – how was that possible? My hands shook – I had to be quick and put everything away.

"Isabel?"

I jerked around, the bottle in one hand, the dripper in the other, the small of my back against the sink. Clara was there, standing in the kitchen. She'd come into the room without a sound – how did she do that?

"Isabel," she repeated, in the saddest tone I'd ever heard. She *knew*. There was no way I could rescue this; there was no way I could pretend I was actually taking those medicines.

I could only say, "I'm sorry."

Clara's face was the picture of disappointment. "Have you been throwing them away all this time?" she asked, in a sad, sad voice. I couldn't take it.

"I . . ." For a second, I contemplated the idea of lying, of arguing my way out of it. But I couldn't. There was no point. I could never convince her not to believe her own eyes.

"Why?"

"Because they're poison. If I take them, I'll get worse. I'll die."

"You can't possibly believe that! You can't possibly believe that your husband would want you to take something poisonous, can you? You think that we want you dead?"

"I don't. I don't believe that. I can't explain . . ."

My hands were shaking so much that the dripper and the bottle fell on the floor and shattered into a million pieces.

"My father always said that's what killed my mum!"

There. I'd said it. In all its absurdity, in all its toxicity, there it was, out into the light. I sat down heavily, shards of glass under my slippers, and took my face in my hands. Clara came to sit beside me and wrapped an arm around my shoulders.

"Oh, Isabel. That's not true. That's not what happened to your mother."

"How do you know?" My face was wet with tears, which were flowing out of my eyes as if they had a will of their own.

Sobs clutched at my chest. Clara did not have an answer for me. She knew nothing. Nobody knew the way my father was. The things he said.

What happened to my mum.

Hardly anybody knew.

What had been passed off as an accident, and wasn't.

"You don't understand, Clara. You really don't. My mum left us. *By choice*." And then it just came out, each word a blade in my heart. "She drowned herself."

I couldn't believe I'd said that.

I couldn't believe I'd given my mum away, revealed her secret, *our* secret, like that. For a moment, Clara felt like a stranger and I felt like a traitor. Why was the sun not darkening? Why did the shards of glass on the floor not embed themselves in my heart? When I had spoken what could never be spoken.

"I'm sorry . . ." Clara whispered. I shook my head.

I'm sorry. How many times have I heard *I'm sorry* since it happened? Said to me, to my sister, to my father – by friends and by the priest and by teachers and by neighbours and by the doctor and by well-intentioned people all around. As if words could ever, ever make it better. As if pretending it had been an accident could ever change the truth.

Nothing could make it better. Not even time, not even growing up.

"You can't possibly *believe* that those medicines are poison."

I was still hiding my face in my hands. I could not speak.

"Isabel. Please. Please tell me what's in your mind. I can help you . . ."

"I don't believe they're *really* poison, but they're bad for me! I tried to take them, but they made me shake, and I was always sleepy, and I had terrible nightmares . . ."

181

"Those are just side effects. If you work through them—"

"How do you know? Have you ever taken them?"

"No, but I wish I had."

And then it all fell into place in my mind. Clara's stories about her friend in distress. The Chinese pills. I looked her in the eye. "It's you, isn't it?"

Silence. And then, "I . . . How . . ."

"The friend you told me about. It's you!"

I saw her taking a breath and her features seemed to relax – for some reason. She nodded.

"Yes. It's me. It *was* me, anyway. And I was on my own, and the doctor just said to take walks in the fresh air, and all I had were those stupid little Chinese pills that did nothing! I wish I'd had proper medication," she said, pointing to the evil little bottle smashed on the floor. "*Please* take your medicines, Isabel. Not for Angus, or for me. Take them for yourself."

"I tried! And I failed every single time, I can't even put them in my mouth! And you can't physically make me," I said, and I cringed at how I sounded like a ten-year-old.

"I have to tell Angus about this. I have to."

"You are blackmailing me now."

"Don't be silly! He deserves to know, Isabel."

"Please don't tell him, he'll just worry!"

"Oh, okay. Because he's perfectly relaxed about the whole thing, isn't he? With you stuck in here," she said, and there was a hint of steel in her voice. It wasn't like her, and I trembled.

"Please, don't tell him," I repeated.

"Oh, Isabel," Clara said, rising from the table and opening the cupboard where I kept the broom and shovel. She began to sweep up the shards. "If only you were a little child and I could *make* you take your medicines."

"But I'm not," I said, my voice now equally steely. "You couldn't ground me, anyway," I added bitterly. "I've grounded myself."

She sighed and dropped the remains of the bottle into the bin. And then she stood there, looking out of the window. I followed her gaze, and we were silent for a while. She looked so weary and her eyes were shiny. I felt so guilty – for a change.

"Look, I . . ."

But she didn't want to talk about it any more. She stopped me with a wave of the hand. "I'll go and get you some more tonight. I know where Angus keeps the prescription," she said curtly, and went to sit in the conservatory.

As soon as Angus arrived, she left without a word. I was afraid she would never come back.

"What's wrong?" Angus asked that night, as we were having dinner. "You are very quiet. And Clara looked strange when I came in."

"Nothing."

"Did you two have an argument?"

"No, no. I'm just tired."

Angus kept studying my face throughout the meal, but he didn't ask again. He went into the study to practise, and I was left alone to think and to berate myself, the music of his violin, for once, failing to soothe me. I was strangely satisfied when, stepping into the kitchen for some tea, I felt a tiny, overlooked shard of glass pierce my bare foot.

36

Dusk

Watch while night falls
Inside my heart

Isabel

I sat at the window in my bedroom, in complete silence but
for the ghost of Angus's music seeping through the wooden
floor from downstairs, like the echo of something long
forgotten, long lost. Tears veiled my eyes as the lilac light of
dusk enveloped the garden and, beyond it, the loch and the
woods. Mist rose from the ground and Venus was bright in the
sky – the landscape was exquisite, but I couldn't appreciate its
beauty.

As day smudged into night, I thought back to all that
my father had told me about my mother's illness, about his
attitude towards medication. The damage that man had done
to me, the damage he'd done to my mum, was immeasurable.

Prayer was what was needed for me, he would have said –
prayer, and pulling myself together. Not that he knew what
was happening to me. I couldn't tell him. I would never tell
him.

The words my father had said about Mum, the words he
had repeated over and over, had become a sort of curse, an

evil spell. They took on more power every time they were repeated, turning a lie into a semblance of truth. The mind of a child couldn't tell the difference.

I knew what he said made no sense. I didn't believe him.

And yet I did.

I had to break the spell he'd cast over me, somehow. The spell *both* my parents had cast over me, something that had waited in silence inside me until one day I pricked myself on the spindle of the spinning wheel. I was the cursed princess in a black fairy tale. Would there be a happy ending for me?

No prince, no knight could save me, even with all the power of his love.

I had to save myself.

To Emer88@iol.ie
From Isabel.C.Ramsay@gmail.com
Clara found out I'm not taking my meds. She hasn't told Angus yet, but she probably will.

To Isabel.C.Ramsay@gmail.com
From Emer88@iol.ie
You're not taking your meds? But Isabel, why? They can make you better! Why, why are you refusing them? It's not because of the crap your father used to say about your mum, is it? I remember him ranting and raving to my parents about the evil of modern psychiatry. What a tosser. Please tell me it's not because of that!

To Emer88@iol.ie
From Isabel.C.Ramsay@gmail.com
I just can't bring myself to take them.

From Emer88@iol.ie
To Isabel.C.Ramsay@gmail.com
That old fart doesn't have a clue, Isabel. He's always been a moron, especially when it comes to you and Gillian. I don't know how your stepmother puts up with him. Please, Isabel. Do it for Angus, do it for me. Take those bloody medicines!

Emer xxx

Outside, the wind was blowing cold and hard. Sometimes the four walls of my house didn't feel like a shelter; they felt like a prison. I was being punished for a crime I had never committed. I wished I could step out into the freezing evening air and let it blow all the pain away. Breathe life into me once again.

That night I dreamt I'd gone outside – I could feel the crackle of dead leaves under my feet; I could see the winter sky above me; I could smell the scent of wind and wet earth. It was so real – and then I woke up, and I was imprisoned once more.

37

Within

I look within
And I still see the little light

Isabel

The woman looking back at me from the mirror the next day was pale, her hair unbrushed, blue bags under her eyes. That woman was me.

I went downstairs slowly, one step at a time. I could hear Angus and Clara talking, and my heart skipped a beat. What was she telling him? Was she telling him about the medication?

I stepped into the kitchen with my heart in my throat.

"All okay, then? I'm off," Angus said, placing a kiss on my cheek.

That was all.

She hadn't told him.

Once Angus had driven away, Clara and I were alone, and it wasn't exactly comfortable companionship. We sat at the kitchen table with our morning coffee, the tension between us palpable. She, too, looked like she hadn't slept much. I could feel her shifting on her chair, preparing to speak, and I was afraid of what she would say.

Maybe she'd tell me that today was her last day. That she would not come back.

"You're not going to stay with me any more, are you?" I said, my eyes low.

I was expecting to be scolded, I was expecting her to tell me how disappointed she was, but she didn't. Instead, she put a hand on mine, in a rush of emotion.

"What? Oh, Isabel. There is no way I would not come back to you," she said softly.

"You look tired."

"So do you. I could barely sleep."

"I'm sorry, I'm so sorry to give you this worry."

"Don't say sorry," she said. "Come on. Let's go to the conservatory and we can talk. We'll sort it all out, you'll see."

We sat among the plants and flowers. The scents were lovely – lavender mixed with the stephanotis and the aromatic herbs, and a strange, almost otherworldly scent of honey. I closed my eyes briefly and opened them again to see Clara looking at me, concern etched all over her face.

"Just . . . tell me. Explain to me why you are not taking your meds; tell me *properly*. Tell me everything, and we can talk it through."

I took a deep breath, cradling the hot coffee in my hands. "It won't work. I just can't do it. I can't take those medicines."

"Why do you say that?" she asked as I took a sip of my coffee. She was so calm. It always seemed to rub off on me.

"Because I tried. I've been trying all this time . . . I've been trying for weeks."

"You told me your father says the medication is poison."

"Yes. He said that's what killed my mum. She was taking pills that made her feel like she wanted to die. How could she stand to leave us?" I burst out, and suddenly it wasn't about the medication, it wasn't about the medication at all.

It was about my mum. That she had abandoned me when I was too small to even remember her face. When I needed her the most. To think of the mothers who are forced to leave their children because of illness, or war, or poverty – but she chose to do so. A part of me couldn't forgive her. A part of me was still a crying child, lost and left to fend for herself.

"Your mum was sick. It wasn't the pills that killed her. She had an illness, just like you do—"

"You always speak like you know her."

"I can empathise with what she's gone through."

"You recovered," I said.

A short hesitation. "There *is* hope, I promise you."

Another silence while I stroked my hair pensively, smoothing its waves down. "My father always said I'm like my mum. Not Gillian: Gillian is like him. She even *looks* like him . . . The funny thing is, I can't really remember my mum. So I don't know how I'm like her. Apart from little things they told me: her love of art, the colour of her eyes . . . They're like . . ." I struggled to find the words. "Like pieces of a jigsaw that I can't quite put together. Too many pieces missing, I suppose . . ."

"Maybe you can be proud to be like your mum."

"I am. But . . ."

"But?"

"But it's scary. Thinking I could be like her in everything. Including this . . . thing that has taken me. This illness."

"This illness is *something that has happened to you*. This illness is *not* you."

"Really? Because it feels like there's nothing left of me." I took a breath, inhaling the sweet scent of honey. And then, like water gushing through a broken dam, all the words that had

189

been choking me finally came out. I was ready to tell my story. "I suppose, looking back, the signs have always been there. I mean, the signs that I was going to be like this, one day. I used to get very upset about little things that shouldn't have worried me much, that didn't worry other children much. Like . . . Oh, it'll seem stupid to you."

"No, tell me."

"Well . . ." I tucked a tendril of hair around my ear. It was difficult to speak up. As if my secret sorrow was a thing of shame. Not even Angus knew everything.

"I was afraid most of the time. Of silly things. Like . . . in my school, we were made to eat whatever we were given. And some days there was food I hated, like, say, cauliflower cheese. When it was time to line up for lunch, we would find out what was on offer that day. I used to worry so much before we got to the dinner ladies, my tummy would cramp, my heart would go crazy. I can see now how my panic was just . . . strange. Sort of out of proportion to what was really happening. I was scared of my teachers, scared of other children, scared of my own shadow. Was just . . . terrified. I tried to tell my dad, but every time I was upset about something he just told me to get on with it, and he was right, I suppose. Except I couldn't . . ."

"He wasn't right. A child is not supposed to just 'get on with it'. You deserved help and comfort. You were only little!"

"I was sure my mum would have understood me. But she wasn't there. So every day I went to school in terror and I couldn't tell anyone." I looked down at my hands. The blade cutting me inside, again. "Sometimes I got so scared about things I couldn't breathe."

190

"I'm so sorry, Isabel."

"It wasn't always terrible, of course," I hastened to add. "I had lots of friends and I loved drawing and reading and climbing trees and playing with my dolls . . . I wasn't always a miserable child. Not on the outside. Just . . . there was a part of me nobody knew about. I kept it secret. I swallowed it down. I thought it would never come up again. But it did."

"But you didn't let it destroy you. You had such a difficult start in life . . . and you still studied art, you married Angus . . . You built yourself a great life. Most people don't achieve half of what you have! You are an illustrator, you work for publishers all over the world . . ."

"Worked. Past tense."

"You're doing something for yourself, now. *Chrysalis*."

"Yes, but that's not the point," I looked at my hands again. Those hands that used to hold a pencil and a paintbrush with such passion, such enthusiasm. "My life has . . . imploded. I can't explain, Clara. One day it was like a switch going on, and that was it. I couldn't switch it back off. I began to feel frightened of everything again. Everything. It's difficult to explain . . ." I repeated.

"There is no need to explain. I think I know what you mean."

"People say 'snap out of it', 'pull yourself together', as if I have a choice. Just imagine, if you were about to be hit by a car. That moment of pure terror, where you think you're going to die. Then multiply it by forever. This is how I live. Nearly every instant of my day."

"Well, that is how a person *should* live," she said.

I was astounded. "What? Why should anyone live like this?"

"Fear is natural, even useful." She shrugged. "It's just that usually we keep it in the back of our minds, otherwise we wouldn't be able to live. We would go crazy."

"How is a state of fear *natural?*"

"What I mean is . . . these bodies we live in are so fragile. We could get sick any moment. Something terrible might be developing inside us right now and we wouldn't have a clue. Bones are easy to break; flesh is easy to burn and mangle . . . You might be doing something as simple as getting a bowl out of a cupboard and before you know it an oven dish falls on your head and you die, all because you wanted to make a shepherd's pie."

For a moment I must have looked like I had no idea what she was talking about. And then I had to laugh, even in my upset.

"Shepherd's pies are bad for you, I *always* knew that."

She smiled back and shook her head. "What I'm trying to say is that *everything* is a dangerous business. I was at the stables yesterday, up at Ramsay Hall . . ."

I felt a stab of longing, thinking of Ramsay Hall, thinking of the horses. Especially Torcuil's mare, Stoirin, the beautiful honey-coloured horse I used to ride.

Thinking about Torcuil, his easy companionship. His constant, steadfast presence . . .

"I watched the riders on their horses. Thinking how easy it would be for them to break their necks. In a single moment. And still, you never think about that. You're sort of aware of it, somewhere in your consciousness. But it's never at the forefront of your mind, otherwise nobody would go horse riding, or do much else, for that matter."

"Exactly! A part of me always felt like that, but I just got on with things. Now, I can't any more. I just can't, Clara. I'm so afraid. All the time."

192

"You know what I think?"

"What?"

"That if you take your medication, if you manage to follow the therapy like the doctor advised . . . Just how it came, this . . . monster you're fighting will leave you."

I shook my head. "It's never going to go."

"Then maybe you have to learn to live with it . . . keep it in its place. Slap it down when you need to. But still live your life. You can do that."

"My mother couldn't. It killed her. She didn't want to live any more, not even for me and my sister."

"Then don't follow in her footsteps. Be stronger. Fight harder."

"You sound like a Nike ad. *Just do it.*" I shrugged my shoulders and looked into my cup. "I don't think I can," I added feebly. I had no fight left. I had used it all just to stay alive, to keep breathing.

"But *I* think you can. And so does Angus. If your mum was still here . . . if your mum could see you now . . ."

"She'd be so disappointed in me."

"Oh, Isabel, that is not true! If she could see you now she'd be so proud of all you've done in your life. She would look after you. She would help you get better . . ."

"Well, she's not, is she?" I said in anger. All of a sudden I felt overwhelmed, nearly nauseated by the conversation. "I'm going upstairs. Sorry, Clara . . ."

"Isabel, wait. We need to talk about the medication. We need to make a plan."

"I'm sorry," I repeated. "It's not going to happen."

Her expression filled me with guilt as I rushed away, to the safe haven of my bedroom.

To Isabel.C.Ramsay@gmail.com
From Emcr88@iol.ic

So, it doesn't look so good with the French guy. When we came back from India, he flew over to Ireland with me, and it was great. For the first couple of days. Then he sort of realised that I really am blind, that it's not a stage gimmick – the blind harpist and all that. I mean, he knew, of course, but he didn't realise how much it affects my daily life. He realised I walk with a white stick, and believe me, there were things I wanted to do to him with that stick after two days! He treated me like I was completely useless. Like I couldn't even blow my nose by myself. Short of cutting my food and feeding me, he behaved like I was a toddler. I just told him to go. Let's face it, I'll never find anyone. Thankfully Donal was at hand with some ice cream and some good music, God bless him.

Tell me about you.

Emer xxx

To Emer88@iol.ie
From Isabel.C.Ramsay@gmail.com

Oh, Emer, I'm so sorry. The French guy sounds like a real pain. Donal is always there when you need him, isn't he? Emer, have you ever tried considering him as more than a friend? Because I know and you know he has had a terrible crush on you since you were five.

Isabel

To Isabel.C.Ramsay@gmail.com
From Emer88@iol.ie

Yeah, Donal is a great friend, but nothing more than that. And if you think he has feelings for me, you are SO wrong! I'm like his little sister. And you didn't tell me anything about you.

To Emer88@iol.ie
From Isabel.C.Ramsay@gmail.com
Me? I'm grand.
Isabel xxx

38

Perfumed rain

The story between us
Is two notes and a look

Angus

She walked like she owned the world. There was no shyness
about her. If you had to say one thing about her, you would
say: *She's strong.* There was no doubt in her eyes. That was
Bibi, marching towards me, a smile on her face. She took my
hands and she kissed me on both cheeks, beaming like she had
been waiting for me and for me only.

She hadn't, of course. That was how she greeted everyone.
And it was wrong that I noticed her kissing James, a piano
player, the same way she kissed me, and looking at him with
the same light in her eyes.

But it was me she looked for when the playing got fast and
magical and each and every one of us was lost in the happiness
that, for our breed, could only be found in music. It was my
eyes she searched for, it was my gaze she met, and we looked
at each other as we played.

Afterwards, I avoided her. There was something too
intimate in that moment we shared.

It was something like a betrayal.

That night I was supposed to stay over in Glasgow, but I didn't. I drove home, and arrived late at night, exhausted. I slipped in the bed beside Bell, her warm body against mine, her sweet scent enveloping me as I held her through the night.

39

Roses

Your words on me
Like warm water

Isabel

"Your hair is so beautiful," Clara said to me the next day, her head cocked to one side. I was drawing in my indoor garden, sketching flowers. I was still working on *Chrysalis*, but I still didn't feel strong enough or focused enough to tackle the *Scottish Legends* book. I kept getting emails from my agent, Joanna, until finally I had to be quite clear with her about my health. She knew I wasn't well, but not to what extent. She had no idea I hadn't been able to work for months. To tell her that had been humiliating, but I had no choice. Maybe she had guessed already, anyway.

"But?" I could feel a *but* coming on.

"But it's really dry. It's because it's been growing for so long without being cut. You don't think . . ."

"I'm not having anyone here!" I exclaimed, suddenly anxious.

"No, don't worry. I was thinking of doing it myself, if that's okay? Your hair is so long, and also it's wavy, so I don't need to be a professional to do a decent job."

"Fine then," I said, a bit reluctantly. But I had thought for a while that my hair, once shiny and strong, was growing lacklustre and brittle, falling halfway down my back.

"Don't worry. I used to cut my daughter's hair, and my husband's too. Come, we'll wet your hair. Do you have a pair of sharp scissors?"

"Yes. In the cutlery drawer."

We sat in the indoor garden, me with my hair wet and Clara with her scissors and brush. She began to comb my hair, and I closed my eyes, inhaling the different scents of the plants and flowers and relaxing under Clara's hands. A memory came from somewhere – a long-forgotten memory of my mum combing my hair one day, long, long ago . . .

"You know, Isabel. You're doing so well. I'm so proud of you. You're working again, and soon you'll be able to start taking those medicines. Angus will be amazed at how much progress you've made . . ." she was saying, and her words melted into each other as I listened, pouring on me like warm water.

Yes, I wanted to live. Yes, I wanted to get better. It was a desire so deep, so visceral, something I had carried with me for a long time while I tossed and turned within the confines of my illness. She brushed some hair off my shoulders and I gazed at her face. She was talking about the two of us going for a walk in the woods one day – she really *believed* what she was saying. She believed that one day we would walk in the woods together . . . Maybe go to La Piazza for a cappuccino . . . She believed I could be *normal*.

I felt a little broken piece of me become whole again. Just like that.

I thought that maybe I could believe her. I thought that maybe she was right. One day I would make a good mum, and I would set things right. I would undo what my mum had done to me.

It was something to fight for.

She touched my wet hair gently, cutting and brushing. The memory of my mum brushing my hair, like an echo of long ago, suddenly became stronger, so strong that I almost felt that if I turned around, she'd be there.

"I think my mum didn't really want to leave me," I said suddenly. I had no idea where those words had come from; they just came into my mind.

Clara was silent. She stopped running her fingers through my hair for a moment, then she began again. When she spoke, there was a tiny catch in her voice. "No, I don't think so either. I think wherever she is, she wishes she'd never left you."

My hair was falling gently on the floor, and I started to speak, to say everything I hadn't been able to tell any counsellor, Emer, not even Angus.

"I was three when she died," I began. "My memories of her are . . . vague. Just impressions . . . like a scent of talcum powder and violets, the feeling of soft wool against my cheek, the sound of laughter." I closed my eyes again, trying to recall an image. They were like tiny silvery fish in a rock pool, impossible to grab – I could only gaze at them swimming around. "When I think of her, I feel like a kind of bubble surrounds me, warm and reassuring. And then I sometimes have specific images come to me, like snapshots . . . Dandelions blowing in the wind on a summer's day, the glimmer of a gold ring on the hand holding mine, the tickle of silky hair against my face as she kissed me. Everything is hazy, impossible to grasp or take hold of, and still too tantalising to allow me to let go. I want to remember so badly; I cried so many times, Clara!

Because these snapshots and hazy memories are all I've got. I was so young. I *try* to recall more, and I could, if only I had something of hers. I would have loved to keep her things with me. Or even just a memento. It's all made so much worse by the fact that I have nothing of hers, not even pictures, nothing. All her photographs, all her things, disappeared."

Clara's scissors stopped.

"What?" Now her voice was trembling. "Why?"

"My dad destroyed them," I said, and I felt tears infiltrating my voice. "My mum had no immediate family who would have kept her pictures, and most of her friends from the church didn't want to upset my father, so whatever they had, they never gave us. My aunt – my dad's sister – died a few years ago, and there was nothing of my mother's among her things. I often asked Gillian, growing up, to tell me what she looked like. She always claimed she couldn't remember. It was a lie, of course, but she always seemed angry when I asked her about Mum, so I stopped. There was always a black cloud around her memory, swallowing everything that had been left – what she looked like, the things she used to say, the way she was. Her taste in things, her fears, her favourite food to eat, what she liked to do and what she couldn't stand – I know *nothing* of these things."

"So you know nothing about her. You've never seen a picture of her," she said. She sounded horrified. I could feel her distress running through me.

"No. I don't. For many years I thought that my father and my sister missed her so much that they couldn't speak about her, they couldn't bear to look at her photograph, so they had swept away every trace of her. So that they wouldn't suffer even more. It was only much later that I found out the real

201

reason for this ... *purge* of her memory, and why Gillian always seemed angry when I asked her about Mum. She wasn't angry at *me* – she was angry at *her*. Because it was not an accident. Her death, I mean. It wasn't an accident."

"That's what you were told at the beginning?" she whispered. She put the scissors down on one of the wicker chairs.

"Yes. We were on holiday in Perthshire, and that's when she disappeared. They told me she went out on the loch and then she fell off the boat on a misty autumn day. It was only when I was six that my dad told me she had loaded her coat pockets with stones and she had let the paddles sink. She had chosen a cold day, so cold that she couldn't have changed her mind and swum back to shore. She let herself fall over the edge of the boat into the freezing water." I felt tears forming in the back of my throat, but I continued. I had this unstoppable need to let it all out. "Often, at night, I see her floating, her eyes open to the sky, her hair in a fan around her face. I wake up and start playing little films to myself, meant to comfort me for a little while, but they end up hurting me even more. But I can't stop. I imagine Gillian stopping her from going out; I imagine myself clinging to her legs, and her picking me up and saying, 'Of course I'm not going, how could I have ever thought of leaving you, my love?' and changing her mind at the last minute. I imagine my father going after her on the loch, taking her in his arms, emptying her pockets full of stones into the water and bringing her back to us. I imagine her struggling in the water, and a fisherman spotting her and saving her, wrapping a blanket around her shoulders to warm her up and saying, 'My God, what a lucky coincidence I was here today! How lucky I spotted you in spite of the mist! You could have easily died!'"

I didn't mention the last little scenario I'd created for myself, the cruellest, the most hopeless of all: that she had drowned, and she was floating, tangled in the reeds along the shore, but an angel took pity on her and breathed life back into her. And she would untangle the algae from her hair and shiver and run as fast as she could along the shore, and back to us.

I took a deep breath. I couldn't feel Clara's hands in my hair any more. I couldn't hear her breathing. She was perfectly still and silent. "But none of this happened," I concluded. "Nobody stopped her, nobody saved her. So that's why my father and my sister have whitewashed her from our lives: yes, they missed her, but they also hated her. I can see it now. They hated her for what she did. And they hated me for loving her, for wanting her. For being like her. For years I dreamt of snow and ice, endless plains of white and cold, because I felt so alone." I couldn't stop talking. Everything I'd kept inside for so long was coming out in one big gush, and I couldn't help it.

"One of my earliest memories is my dad shushing me. He did it all the time: after school, at the weekends, especially on a Sunday, when it was time to go to church and only think about holy matters. When I was growing up, the house was always silent. My dad didn't like noise. Once, someone from the church told me that when my mum was alive the place was always full of people and music. She loved music: I used to try to sneak a listen with my CD player every time my dad wasn't around, also to feel closer to her . . . I often wonder, if my dad hadn't been so religious, would he have been more compassionate towards what my mum did? Maybe he would have made an effort to understand her unhappiness, to love her more, to love her better . . ."

A strangled sound stopped me. I turned around to see that Clara's face was wet with tears.

"Clara! Oh, Clara, please don't cry!" I felt terrible. I couldn't believe my words had upset her so much.

"I'm so sorry . . ."

I held her in my arms, my wet hair everywhere – she still smelled of Christmas, I thought, just like when she'd come to me in that dream. How weird, I thought, for me to be comforting someone instead of the opposite. How selfish illness can make you, when you think you're the only one who ever has needs.

So our roles were reversed and I held her as she cried and I felt her wet tears on my cheek. And then something weird happened: we looked into each other's eyes, and I noticed they were so similar – nearly the same green.

"I'll tell you what we are going to do," I said. "I'll make us some hot chocolate and we can have some cake and we'll feel better, okay?" I smiled inwardly at the role reversal. Clara sat down, and I went to prepare the hot chocolate. I left it on the stove bubbling away on a low heat, and I thought I'd go and get a towel for my wet hair.

I was back a minute later. And in a split second I thought, *Yes, I should have got that gas ring seen to, I should have called someone to repair it sooner rather than later*, because the flame had burnt wonky, as it tended to do, and had set a kitchen towel on fire, and the flames danced stronger and stronger by the second – now everything would burn, burn. I was mute and frozen in horror.

40

Fire

Watch with me
The deadly dance
of my destruction

Isabel

I should have got out at once. I should have got Clara by the arm and run out with her into the garden without looking back ... It's what they teach you as a child: if you see fire, don't try to be a hero, just run for your life.

But I didn't.

In that instant of panic I couldn't think clearly, and I threw my towel on the stove, trying to suffocate the fire licking up from the stove, dancing beautiful and deadly, higher and higher, the flames' blue roots turning red and orange. Black smoke began to fill the room. A gust of flames blew sudden and scorching in my face, and I jerked backwards. I tripped on a chair and fell to the ground, banging the back of my head so hard I saw stars. Tears from the smoke were falling down my face, and I struggled to keep my eyes open – I knew I had to get up fast, because the fire was spreading and the smoke was turning thicker and more toxic by the minute. As I lay on the kitchen floor, my head swimming, I saw the flames engulf their surroundings – the tablecloth and the curtains. All of a sudden there was fire everywhere, all the oxygen sucked out of the room by the hungry flames. It was all happening so quickly – all I could think was I had to get up before I was set on fire myself, before my lungs burnt with the scalding smoke. But my limbs wouldn't answer. My head felt wet, and when I felt my hair with my fingers, I saw that they were red with blood, but I didn't know where it was coming from. My head pounded. *Get up! Get up!*

Then someone shouted my name, and Clara was crouching beside me, and we couldn't breathe, and I wanted us to crawl out into the corridor and outside to safety, but all of a sudden the smoke was so thick I couldn't see any more. Clara was coughing hard, and her breaths were more and more laboured – she was suffocating. I tried to yell at her to go and leave me, but my throat was too dry and sore to speak. I tried to get up, with Clara helplessly dragging my arm upwards, but my legs would not support my weight – I could only sit up, leaning against Clara. She wrapped her arms around me, her chest shaken by fits of coughing, and I shut my eyes for a moment – but then instinct kicked in and my body decided for itself what to do. I freed myself from Clara's embrace and managed to twist my body so that I was on all fours – I began crawling towards the door, making sure Clara was beside me. We managed only a few inches when she collapsed in a coughing fit. I could not go without her, and I didn't have the strength to drag her with me. So I stopped, and a part of me whispered in my mind: *It's all over.* Funny. Now that life was going to be taken away from me, I wanted to live more intensely than ever. How ironic that I should die like this, not by my own hand but because of something as banal as a malfunctioning gas ring.

How fragile is life, how precious.
And now it's all about to end.
Goodbye, Angus.

I closed my eyes and I prayed it would be quick, for me and for Clara. Her fingers found mine – we held each other's hand, and I felt my consciousness ebb away . . . Then a strong arm took me and dragged me across the floor, and out of my half-closed eyes I saw the sky. I was outside. I was saved. *Clara,* I thought at once, and I must have called her name because someone answered, "She's here, she's fine." Relief swept through me as something gripped my stomach and I vomited on the grass, long hard retches that left me sore and trembling. I turned my head slowly, painfully, and there she was – Clara beside me, still coughing so hard it sounded like barking. I gazed at the sky.

It was blue.

Someone held me in his arms. His chest smelled familiar; his grip was strong, nearly painful; a sob wrecked his chest. *It must be Angus,* I thought. *My love, you came to save me.* And so I whispered, "I love you."

But it was Torcuil's voice that answered. He called my name over and over and over again.

And then the ambulance came.

41

The time we turn around

When all I hold dear
Could dissolve in a heartbeat
That is the moment
I can only call for you

Angus

Torcuil was distraught, his hands shaking as he held a glass of water. Bell and Clara owed him their lives. Which meant I owed him my life too.

He was there to save Bell. I wasn't.

I was working. As always. He'd driven to the cottage as soon as he'd seen the black smoke rising and arrived before the fire brigade and the ambulance. His face was black with oily smoke, and there was a burn on his left hand. He had refused to have that seen to, but they had bandaged it anyway, despite his protestations that it was nothing.

"Isabel couldn't get out. She was lying on the floor, there was blood on her head . . . I couldn't see much, the smoke was burning my eyes . . ." He opened his arms. "Clara could walk, but she wouldn't go anywhere without Bell, she was just crouching there beside her . . . She could walk, she *could*. She could have walked out," he repeated, as if he could not believe what had just happened. It was all surreal.

"Clara risked her life for Bell?"

"Yes. As soon as I began dragging Bell out, Clara followed. She collapsed there," he said gesturing to my doorstep. "You should have heard the way she was coughing, it was like a bark. I thought she would suffocate. The smoke was so thick my throat was burning, and I'd only been inside for a minute or two. I don't know how she . . . how she switched off her survival instinct. She would not leave without Izzy. Simple as that. I just don't know how we can ever thank her."

"I don't know how to thank *you*, Torcuil," I said, looking away to the still waters of the loch. I paused. "I need to ask you a question." Did I? Did I need to know? Did I need to find out if Izzy could not get out, or refused to get out? If she had wanted to stay in and let herself suffocate. That would have worked. Unlike the pills, that would have worked.

"She couldn't move. She was nearly unconscious, though not quite." Torcuil read my mind, like he often did.

"So you don't think . . ."

"I don't know. No. No, I think it was an accident, Angus. I don't know how the fire started, but she was hurt, she couldn't walk, she couldn't even crawl. She couldn't have got out by herself."

"Okay. Okay," I said, and I realised I was shaking too.

"I'm not doing enough for Izzy. I'm just not doing enough . . ." Torcuil burst out.

A pang of jealousy hit me. He had been there to save her life. And he claimed he wasn't doing enough for her. He was her brother-in-law, for God's sake, how much was a brother-in-law supposed to do?

Unless he was more. Unless he still felt he was more, to her.

"It's not up to you, Torcuil. It's up to me to help her," I said, and wondered what kind of small-minded person would come out with something so petty at a time like this. I was ashamed of myself.

And then something changed on Torcuil's mellow, kind features – and he snapped. He looked like he was about to say something, then he stopped.

But then: "But you aren't, are you? You are *not* here, Angus. Like you weren't there when our father was dying. Because you're always somewhere else. Always busy with your music. Sometimes I really think nothing else matters, for you. Nothing."

I watched Torcuil's face turn twisted and contorted in rage, and I couldn't believe what I'd just heard.

Or maybe I could. Because it was the truth, yes – it was the truth. But it was something I had always pushed to the back of my mind, something I'd always found excuses for. Nobody had ever spelled it out to me so clearly, so cruelly.

Of course. It was all my fault.

I had let Bell down.

I had let everybody down.

Me and my music: my wife, my mother, my lover, my best friend, my life.

But I was only human and, together with contrition, came rage.

"I left Bell with Clara! I thought she was being looked after! And if I remember correctly, it was you pushing so much for me to hire Clara. Because you had a vision, a good feeling. You didn't see the fire, did you? Your crystal ball didn't tell you that!"

"Who says it was Clara's fault? And she refused to leave Izzy."

"Isabel! *She is Isabel to you.*"

Suddenly, Torcuil looked deflated. All the anger swept from him, and he held his left arm in his right hand. I could see him trembling.

I couldn't look him in the face any more. "Do you still have feelings for her, Torcuil?" I said in a low voice, in a way that was almost soft.

There was a pause, while he winced in pain – his hand, I supposed.

"Of course not. I love her like a sister. That is all."

I said nothing.

"I'm sorry. I'm sorry for what I said," he murmured.

"It's true."

He shook his head.

"It isn't. I was just angry."

It was too painful to keep discussing it. I didn't want to hear what he had to say.

I couldn't.

"You need to get that hand seen to."

"It's nothing. I have some burn cream at home."

"It might not be enough, they might want to—"

"Look, I'll leave you to get on with things . . ." He gestured towards upstairs, where Isabel was lying down. She somehow convinced the firemen that she was fine and they let her stay. Clara, instead, was in hospital. Torcuil turned away and walked off without any more words, without a backward glance. I had a bitter taste in my mouth as I watched him step out of my garden and disappear.

He might have just saved Bell's life, getting here before the firemen, and all I could do was be jealous. Because he had shown concern for my wife.

I was ashamed.

And still, there was something in his eyes, when he spoke about Isabel.

Izzy.

I strode upstairs two steps at a time, the acrid smell of burnt wood and plastic in my nostrils, my eyes still streaming though the smoke was long gone. The stuff was poisonous, oily, adhering to skin and clothes like soot. Bell was sitting on the bed, her hair lanky and blackened, but her face cleaned where the paramedics had checked for burns. Her left forearm was bandaged.

"Why, Bell?" I could only yell. "Why did you do it?"

"I didn't start the fire on purpose—"

"I know! I know you wouldn't go that far! But you refused to get out. Did you actually want to die in that fire?" God help me, I wanted to smack her for having done what she'd done. If I had to be damned for it, I wanted to smack her for having just sat there, waiting for the smoke to kill her. And kill Clara too.

"No! No way! I promise you! I didn't want to die! I hadn't felt that way since . . . since Clara arrived."

"Well you seem to really care for her, considering you nearly got her killed! She wouldn't leave your side! Torcuil had to prise her off you!"

She hung her head. "I'm so sorry."

"She is in hospital, Isabel. Because of you." I said, and immediately I hated myself for it. But the fear and despair and the terrible, terrible rage I'd felt for the last two years was exploding in me.

"I'm so sorry," she sobbed again.

"Then why didn't you get out?" I was aware that I was shouting, that I was scaring her. I'd never thought I could be that person, shouting at my wife – but I couldn't help it, I couldn't stop.

"I was scared!"

"You were more scared of being out of the house than suffocating or burning? Are you crazy?"

"I suppose I am, yes," she murmured.

And then all the fight went out of me. I knelt in front of her, like a desperate supplicant, and I took her hands.

"Bell. Once and for all, tell me the truth." She looked at me. "Did you try to do it again?" There was no need to specify what *it* was.

She locked her eyes on mine. "No. No. I was terrified; I didn't want to die. I don't want to die."

"Well, you nearly did. For the second time. We can't keep going on like this, Bell."

"What do you mean?"

I took a deep breath. "I don't know. I don't know what I mean. But maybe . . ."

And suddenly, unexpectedly, she threw herself into my arms and I held her, like a frightened animal. I held her tight, tight, I never wanted to let her go.

"Maybe what?"

"Maybe you need to go somewhere you'll be safe."

All of a sudden, she went rigid in my arms.

"No! No! I'm safe with you! It was an accident . . ."

"But it would be for your own good. Bell, I need your help here. I swear, I don't know what to do any more. I just don't know what to do."

"Keep me with you. Give me one more chance. Just one more chance."

I just held her, and cried in her hair.

213

42

It's you I love

You used to love me once,
How could it ever change?

Torcuil

Margherita was looking at me, thinking I couldn't see her. I'd been lost in thought, looking out at our garden, asleep for winter. Waiting.

Like us.

Waiting for Izzy to get better.

"Something on your mind?"

"Nothing."

"There's something bothering you, I can tell," I insisted gently.

"It's nothing, really."

I raised my eyebrows.

"It's just . . . sometimes I worry."

"What do you worry about?"

"It's difficult to put into words . . ." She looked almost embarrassed. At that moment, I knew what she wanted to talk to me about, and I prepared my answers.

"Try . . ." I took a chair and placed it in front of her at the kitchen table. I took both her hands, locking my eyes on hers. "Tell me."

"That you still love her," she blurted out.

For a moment, my stomach clenched. How could I explain? How could I explain that someone you loved once would never be out of your heart – and it meant everything and nothing, because life moved on and things changed and a heart didn't cling to what it had lost, like a barnacle on a rock. The heart changed too, and mine had. And hadn't.

And Isabel's was in a similar limbo, because the words she'd said to me when I saved her from the fire told me so.

How could I explain?

"I do love her . . ." I began – her eyes widened – "but not like that. Not like I used to. The place she used to have . . . You have it now."

"Are you sure? Because I couldn't take it. It would break my heart."

"I'm sure. Margherita, it's you I love. And you only," I said, and I was grateful. Grateful she was safe, grateful she was healthy. Grateful, as selfish as it may sound, that we didn't share the same predicament as Angus and Izzy.

"It's you I love," I repeated, holding her and breathing in her scent of soap and sugar.

43

Don't take her away

If one day I was to find you again
I would pray every God in the sky
Please don't take her away

Angus

An uneasy truce was simmering between me and my brother. When we walked in, Clara was sitting on the hospital bed and combing her brown-grey hair. I was relieved beyond words to see she had no oxygen mask, no line, none of those scary things you see on TV. She was even wearing her own clothes, sitting with her back straight, her movements calm and measured.

"Sorry. Is it a bad moment?"

"No, come in, come in." Her voice was a bit hoarse, but apart from that and being quite pale she seemed unscathed. "The nurse lent me a comb. I must look a fright." Her serene smile, once more.

"Not at all," I said clumsily.

"How are you feeling?" asked Torcuil, placing the flowers we'd brought down on her bedside table.

"Like I want to get out of here!" she laughed, then coughed a little. Suddenly I realised that her cheeks were very pink – she must have been given oxygen. "They said Isabel is at home. What a relief!"

"Yes. She had a bad bump on her head, but no burns, and her lungs are fine. All in all she was extremely lucky. I'm sorry—" I began, but she interrupted me.

"There is nothing to apologise about. It really was just an accident. Isabel was trying to make hot chocolate for me."

I exchanged glances with my brother.

"Is that what happened?"

"Yes. I know, I was there! We had noticed that a gas ring was faulty. We should have sent for Dougie at once, but it slipped both our minds." Of course. How could I have thought that Bell had something to do with this? It made no sense. But I still had a terrible doubt in my mind.

"She couldn't move, could she? That's why she didn't get out."

"That's right. When I arrived she was lying on the floor and there was blood on her head and her face. It was horrible . . ."

"You stayed with her. You refused to leave her," Torcuil murmured.

"Well. I couldn't leave her, could I?"

I was left speechless by her loyalty.

"Angus. We need to talk." Clara was looking straight at me, eyes on mine. She never looked down, or away – she held another person's gaze like she was always unafraid and unashamed.

"Is there something you haven't told me, Clara?"

"She *hasn't* been taking her medication," Clara blurted out. "She has been throwing it away."

Floor and ceiling swapped places for a moment, then the world rearranged itself, but it was a strange world, a world I didn't know any more.

"*What?*"

"I'm sorry, I—"

217

"And you didn't think of telling me!" I struggled to keep my voice low. This was a hospital, but I was seeing red.

"I only found out two days ago. Believe me, I was as shocked and as angry as you are. But confronting will solve nothing. I'm trying to reach her slowly—"

"We need to step up a gear," I said, trying to sound hard but sounding terrified instead.

Clara's face fell. "What do you mean?"

"We need a nurse. I mean, a *psychiatric* nurse. We need to . . . step up a gear," I repeated lamely.

"But . . . but I have a plan! And it's working! Slowly, but it's working!"

"If things are working so well, why did you feel the need to tell me about the meds at all?"

"Because I realised I shouldn't have kept it from you. And I'm so sorry I did . . ."

"You're sorry you kept it from him or you're sorry you told him?" Torcuil said cryptically.

"What do I employ you for, if you're not checking on her—"

"Angus!" Torcuil snapped.

And then I remembered. I remember that Clara hadn't run out of a burning building, so she could remain with my wife.

"I'm sorry. I'm sorry, Clara."

"She will take her medicine. I promise you. Please, give me a chance to let this work. Let me do what I need to do."

"And what would that be?" I said, more harshly than I would have liked. But I couldn't help it.

A hesitation. "Help her get better."

"Will you see she takes her medicines?" I'd been deceived all that time. It couldn't happen again.

"Yes," she said, and looked me straight in the eye again. She was on the verge of tears.

"I want her to take her pills every morning in front of me if I'm there, or in front of you. Is it a deal?"

"Yes," she repeated.

Suddenly, Torcuil opened his mouth, like he was about to say something.

I looked at him. We both did. And then something passed between him and Clara, a secret communication I wasn't part of.

And then he said something unexpected. "Don't worry, Clara. You won't be separated."

"Well, what can I say? She's like a daughter to me."

A moment of silence, then I spoke. "So, how long do you have to stay in hospital? Is there anything we can do?"

"They say they'll let me out after the afternoon rounds. I'll take a taxi back."

"No way, I'll come and get you," Torcuil offered.

"There's no need . . ."

"Please. Honestly, it's no bother."

"What about your hand?"

"My hand is okay."

"If you come and get Clara," I intervened, "I'll be able to stay with Bell."

"Like I said, it's no problem. Clara . . . thank you. For not leaving her, I mean." Torcuil gave her a brief hug and she returned it with warmth, like a mother. I looked on, too wound up, too wrapped in my worry to be part of their connection.

I mumbled a goodbye. I was confused, torn between gratitude and anger, overwhelmed by this whole mess, unable to say anything more.

We walked to the hospital car park and my head pounded with tension.

"Torcuil, I think I missed half of that conversation. What did you and Clara *say* to each other? I mean, the way you looked at each other . . . What was all that about?"

"What do you mean?"

"You know what I mean. It's like . . . she told you something. Or you told her something. Without words."

"I'm not telepathic, Angus."

"No, but you seem to *know* . . . I can't explain."

"I know that we have to let Clara try. I'm sorry if you think my feeling misled you, but I'm convinced that hiring Clara was the right thing to do."

A fine drizzle was falling from the sky, tossed about by the wind, chilling me to the bone. Pewter clouds weighed on me from above.

"I understand," I said, but it wasn't entirely true. I don't always understand what goes on in Torcuil's mind, but in spite of what I said during our argument, I certainly trust him. Truth is, I trust him with my life, and trust is more important than understanding.

"If things don't change, we'll think about it then," he said – and again, his use of *we* riled me a little.

"I need to think about this now, Torcuil. I want to give Clara another chance, but maybe a psychiatric nurse . . . I can't believe Isabel hasn't been taking her medication! I'm so angry I can't even . . ." I rubbed my forehead with shaking hands. The pain in my head was getting stronger, nausea lingering at the edges of my awareness.

"I know," Torcuil replied, taking my car keys gently from my hand and opening the door of my Mini. "Come on. Get inside. I'll take you home."

"Why? Why on earth is she refusing to get better?" I said in frustration as Torcuil started the engine.

"She has her own logic, and it makes sense to her."

"Her logic is warped."

"I know. We need to work together and make her change her mind."

"I want somebody to be with her every single morning when she takes those bloody pills, every single time I'm not there."

Once again Torcuil seemed about to say something, and then changed his mind. "*Clara* will be there," he said instead.

I wish I could be there for her, I heard.

But I wouldn't let myself be overwhelmed with jealousy, not again. I would not cast words at him like stones. Not after the things I'd said to him that morning, only for him to still stand by me. As he always does.

"You really seem to have a lot of trust in her," I said, hoping against hope that Torcuil would elaborate a little about this mysterious *feeling* he had about her.

"I do. I told you. She's a good person."

"Right. She's a good person. And that's the reason why you trust Clara. That's all you have to say on the matter."

"Pretty much." A pause, while I watched the empty grey moors flit by. "Also I know she had a daughter just like Isabel."

His tone made it sound like the conversation was over. As we stopped in front of my house, Torcuil took a deep breath, his eyes closed, and then left without a word.

221

If I lost you

This life is burning,
All my memories
Turning to ash

Isabel

How ironic. A fire started in my house and people thought I'd tried again to top myself. All because I was trying to make hot chocolate for Clara. It gave a whole new meaning to the expression "death by chocolate".

"Did you see Clara?" I asked anxiously as soon as Angus stepped in, while Morag slipped out with a murmured goodbye. Angus went straight to the bathroom and I followed suit, trying not to look at the darkened doorstep of my kitchen. There was less damage than we'd thought; later on, work would begin to clean up and replace the burnt units. I shuddered at the idea of having people in the house, of course, but it could not be helped – and I wanted my kitchen back. I wanted to forget all about what had happened.

"She's okay. I can't believe it, Bell. I can't believe this happened," he said, rummaging in the bathroom cupboard. Finally, he took out a blister pack of something and swallowed two pills, dry.

"Are you okay?"

"Fine. Never been better." He sounded like he hated me. Like he blamed me for the fire.

"Look, Angus, I told you what happened! Clara must have told you too! I had nothing to do with the fire. I was making hot chocolate for Clara and I, and the gas ring—"

"I know," he said, stepping into the living room. He leaned against the mantelpiece, one hand massaging his temple.

"So . . . what is this all about? Why are you looking at me like that?"

"I'm going to phone Dr Tilden and organise hooking you up with the Crisis team." The expression he used. *Hooking me up*. I had a sudden vision of me being pierced in the middle, wiggling on a hook like bait.

"Why? I've been feeling so much better. Every day a little more. And now you want to go and spoil everything . . ."

Angus had his back to me. Just in front of him on the mantelpiece lay a framed picture of our wedding. "Bell. She *told* me."

"What . . . ? Oh."

The medicines. The one secret I'd kept from Angus.

And now it was out.

Silence. I could find no more words to justify myself. Angus turned around, his ice-blue eyes on me with all the weight of his pleading.

"We can't keep going on like this, Bell. Tell me you understand. Tell me you'll work with the Crisis team and—"

"Angus. Please, I'm not recovered yet. But I'm on the right track. If you force me to speak to strangers, I—"

"How can you tell me you're on the right track when you haven't been taking your medication? I'm an idiot for not checking! But you *promised* you would. And you are an adult.

223

I didn't think I had to supervise you like a ten-year-old!"

"I'm sorry." What else was there to say?

"You should be. This not taking meds is the most stupid thing I ever . . ." He began to pace up and down, his arms crossed, his face hard. Tears gathered in my eyes, threatening to spill. "I just don't know what to do any more. I've tried everything. I begged you. And you promised, you promised me—"

"It's my *father!*" I burst out. "It's my father . . ."

He stops in his tracks. "What?"

I shook my head. Angus came beside me and took me by the shoulders. "Bell. Please, talk to me. Tell me. What did your father say to you?"

And now the tears were flowing down my cheeks, unstoppable, unchecked. "He always said the medication killed my mum. The pills made her 'crazy', he used to say."

Angus just stood there, his mouth open.

"Your father said that?"

"Yes."

"And you believed him?"

"I was a little girl, Angus. I didn't know any better. And then when I got sick . . . his words came back to me, and . . ."

Before I knew it, he'd taken me in his arms.

"My poor, poor Bell. Your father was talking nonsense, do you hear me? It was him who needed treatment, for God's sake! I can't believe you've had to carry this on your shoulders for so long. Had I known . . ." I could feel him trembling with anger. "Well, I know, now. And we are going to sort this together. I promise."

"Please don't phone Dr Tilden. I really am on the right track . . ."

He pushed me away gently, so he could look me in the eyes.

"Fine. But you know what I'm going to say."

"You're going to say that there will be no more excuses, now. That I have to take my pills."

"Yes. I promise you that what your father said is nonsense. Complete nonsense. God, *your father* was the sick one! Not your mum!"

Those words were too painful to reply to.

Because I had come to wonder that too.

That if my mum had had the right support, the right help, she'd be alive today, but all she'd got from her husband was blame.

She didn't have any of that, but I did. I had a chance. And I had to take it.

"I'll be there when it's time to take your pills. And when I'm not, I'll ring Clara, at nine on the dot, no matter what . . . unless I'm in the middle of playing – in that case I'll ring the second I'm finished."

"Okay."

"Okay?"

"Yes. Yes." I was going to say "I promise", but I had promised before and it hadn't worked out. No more promises. I would just do it.

"I'm not going to Prague." Angus was due to go to the Czech Republic with the orchestra. "I can't leave you, not this time."

To my shame, I was relieved.

And then I realised the implications of it.

He couldn't miss such an important concert. I couldn't allow it. I couldn't have the guilt of wrecking his career on my shoulders, on top of everything else.

Angus was looking down. And then he raised his head and gazed at me with eyes that said, *Please, say I can go.*

I knew him too well.

"You need to go."

"But—"

"You need to go. Angus, we both know that if I try to keep you here with me all the time you'll be miserable. You need to do your work. You need to play your music. We can't have it any differently. You can't have it any differently, and neither can I, because when I married you I knew this was the deal."

"But you weren't ill, then."

"And I won't always be. Please, go to Prague. We'll do the phone thing, won't we? Every morning at nine, and if you can't, as soon as you're finished. I'll take my medication. Clara will be here. We'll get through this."

"Yes. We'll get through this."

And then I looked up, just for a moment.

I looked up to the ceiling – through the layer of bricks and mortar lay all my dreams. My studio. My work.

Because Angus wasn't the only one who had a passion in our little family. Except I had nearly lost mine. And it could never happen again.

And so he left, in the middle of the night. He kissed me softly and we murmured a goodbye, and then he was gone. Clara was sleeping in the spare room. Later on, the workmen would come and restore the kitchen to order.

Clara and I were to be alone for four days. The worst thing for me was thinking of her hurt, in a hospital bed. And that it had been my fault.

"You were hurt, pet," she said to me as we sat in the

conservatory, the lushness of my plants and flowers against the backdrop of the barren winter scene. "And I know it was an accident, I was there, remember? We were just trying to make hot chocolate and that gas ring was faulty. We both knew it and neither of us called Dougie to fix it. So it's both our faults."

"I know," I said, still consumed by guilt. "But you could have run out and you wouldn't have ended up in hospital."

"And leave you there? No. But maybe now I'm in a position to ask you to do something for me."

"Of course. I'll do anything. Anything to make amends. I'm so—"

"No. No more *I'm sorry*. This is what we're going to do. I spoke with Angus; he said he's going to call me every morning at nine. So I've set the alarm on my phone to ring at exactly eight thirty. At that time, every morning, you and I will try to take the meds. I'll be here to help you." She disappeared into the hall and came back with a Boots bag. She lined up the medicines on the low wicker table, right in front of me, deliberately. A dark little bottle, replacing the one I'd broken, and a white box labelled with my name and address.

I took a breath so deep it seemed to come from my toes. I looked at my watch. A quarter to nine.

I had to do it.

Though I thought those things would poison me, I had to take them, because I'd always tried to do it all myself, without help – and look at all that had happened. I couldn't make it by myself: it was as simple as that. I needed help. And help was there for me, there for the taking. I didn't have to keep fighting alone. If only I could overcome this one obstacle, it would be a new beginning.

Clara poured me two glasses of fresh water, and then sat across from me, still and silent, with her usual serenity. Without a word, I opened the bottle and dosed the right amount carefully, drop by drop. I brought the glass to my lips – my hand was trembling. I closed my eyes for a moment.

This won't kill you. It won't poison you.

This will save you.

And so I drank.

I felt panic unfurl in my stomach, the monster about to bite me and send me into a world of pain – Clara was holding her breath as I swallowed the last gulp, and then, finally, she let herself sit back in the chair with a barely perceptible sigh.

I ignored the monster. I closed my eyes to it; I closed my ears to it. As much as it screamed and clawed at me to listen, I ignored it. And my father's voice, I ignored that too – no, I would not pay heed to what he had said.

"I've done it," I said, the sickly taste of the drops in my mouth.

"Not yet. You have to do this every morning," Clara said mercilessly. "The doctor said you're going to feel a small difference after two weeks. And after six weeks, I promise you, things will be a lot better then."

Six weeks? Six weeks of this, every morning. And more. My heart pounded – the monster uncoiled its spikes, and I was afraid, so very afraid.

"Is that a deal?" she insisted.

I nodded, at a loss for words.

And then I threw myself into her arms and I breathed in her scent of lavender and talcum powder and Christmas, and she rocked me gently as I cried and cried.

"Oh, Isabel," she said with that soft voice of hers, that calming, comforting voice. "I'm so proud of you."

And for once in my life, instead of feeling guilty or ashamed or inadequate – for once in my life, I felt proud of myself too.

Sure enough, the mobile rang at nine on the dot – I jumped out of my skin. "Yes, hello Angus. Yes, she took them both. Right in front of me."

"Tell him I'll text him!" I couldn't speak to him yet. One phobia defeated was enough for one day, in my book. But I would get there. I would use the phone again; I would get out of the house; I would be myself again. All those fears, I would beat them all, one by one.

"She says she'll text." Clara was beaming. "No problem. Speak soon. Bye." Clara put the mobile down triumphantly and I grabbed mine.

I did it!
I took the medicines!
It was hard but I did it. I can't wait to see you.

The reply came at once.

I'm insanely proud of you. I can't wait to see you too.
All my love
A xxxxxxxx

The monster conceded me a moment of happiness.

45

Sunflower

When I stand right
At the edge of the abyss

Angus

It felt wrong to leave Bell when she was hurting so much, but I only had a few more concerts left before my trial with the orchestra was finished. If I held on long enough, if I managed to clear my mind of all worries while I was playing, if I gave my all in spite of what was happening at home – I would make it.

I landed in Prague just in time to call Clara. My heart was in my throat.

"Clara?"

I stood and listened while Clara told me that finally Bell had taken her medicine. The relief was immense. And then Bell's text came – her loving words, her triumph.

We had taken a step. It might have been a small step, but it felt like conquering a new continent.

And there I was, later that morning, sitting in a small coffee shop outside, in the winter sun. We were taking a break after a spot of sightseeing. Bibi held court, as ever. She was beautiful, with a silken sleeveless dress and black sunglasses, and a woollen shawl draped around her shoulders.

"I was in Barcelona for the weekend with a crowd of friends. It was crazy. Really, really good. I'm still catching up on sleep. There was so much to see, so much to do . . . and so much music around, Barcelona is just amazing for that . . ."

As she was talking, I looked at her face – animated, full of life. She made me think of a sunflower, drinking sunlight like she drinks life. But she wasn't just charismatic – there was substance to her. She was a fantastic, dedicated musician and practised like a woman possessed. When she played, she left me speechless.

She reminded me of Isabel.

Before she got sick.

There was something in my heart, a little bloom that I needed to squash. But I couldn't.

I sent Isabel picture after picture, text after text, like a secret, silent apology.

46

Alchemy

The fragile chemistry
of all our minds

Isabel

Cold winds were blowing in from the Atlantic, and I shivered in the morning and sat close to the fire at night. I missed Angus so much. After Prague there had been a few days at home, and then he was away again, to London and a tour of England.

But there was something good. Something so good, I nearly couldn't believe it. For nearly two weeks I'd been taking my medicines religiously. For the first few mornings drinking those drops and swallowing the pill had been a battle, but I'd done it. And then it got easier and easier, until it was nearly as natural as drinking my coffee.

And I could feel the change in me, as if slowly the chemistry of my mind was changing, as if what had been frayed and fractured was repairing itself, bit by bit, hour by hour, day by day. As if the pieces of my identity, scattered and lost, were coming back together.

One morning I woke up to a grey light streaking in from the window and an empty bed – and as usual, I waited for the familiar hit of panic, for my heart to race like every time a new day began. But it didn't happen. The drops were supposed to relax me, and they did. For the first time in months I felt like my muscles weren't constantly contracted, and so I began to sleep nearly every night: a dreamless, restful sleep that restored my body and my mind.

I blinked over and over again, stretching under the duvet, brushing the hair out of my face. A new day was dawning, and it didn't seem so bad. A parade of soothing thoughts moved through my mind, tentative, like toddlers taking their first steps – sometimes swaying, sometimes falling, but there: it was cold in my room, but the duvet felt lush and comforting around my body – the muted light of winter was beautiful in a calm, sleepy way – a cup of coffee and a chat with Clara were awaiting me downstairs – Angus would be back soon.

I felt *better*.

For the first time in months, years even, I didn't start the day with dejection. It was like a different world, like a veil had been removed from my eyes. The change was subtle and yet so deep it had me sitting up in bed, hugging my knees, feeling wave after wave of relief sweeping over me. Why had I allowed my father's lies to deceive me for so long? Why had I followed the voice of my anxiety instead of listening to the doctor, to Angus, and Torcuil, and Clara, and all those who loved me?

It wasn't joy, not by a long shot, but it was the absence of despair – and it meant everything to me. Instead of shedding tears, I was ready, maybe, to smile.

I threw a cardigan around me and went downstairs. Clara was in the kitchen already. My new, gleaming kitchen was a sight to behold – and having the workmen in the house hadn't been as traumatic as I'd feared. Because Angus had been away, Torcuil had had my illustrations reframed in Kinnear, and they had taken their place again on the kitchen walls.

"Morning!" I said brightly. I could see Clara's face lighting up, mirroring mine.

"'Morning, Isabel. How did you sleep?"

"Very well, thank you," I said, and I sat down in front of the coffee Clara had prepared for me.

I could feel Clara studying me, but I didn't say anything. She took a breath and I thought she'd speak, but she didn't. We were both frightened of breaking the spell of my morning smile, I think.

And then, as I looked out of the kitchen window to the white sky and the frozen ground, where there was a soft white mist draped on the hills – I said it.

"Clara."

"Yes, pet." It was funny how she called me *pet*, though she was only a few years older than me.

"I want to try to go outside."

The moment those words came out, I regretted them – it seemed impossible. Like stepping on a rope bridge, suspended on an abyss and blowing in the wind. And then, I steeled myself. I would at least try. I would try with all I had.

Clara was silent for a moment, and then she smiled. "Let's go, then."

The few steps between the wicker chair and the conservatory door were like a pilgrimage between two wings of scented flowers. I opened the door and stood there, trembling with cold and sheer panic. I could feel Clara's hope, her expectations, as she stood firm beside me, solid, ready to catch me if I turned back and to accompany me if I walked on.

I took a deep breath; the air of early winter, biting my hands

234

and my face, smelled like icy grass. It smelled like the future. I wrapped the cardigan around me tighter and took another breath.

One step. Just one step.

And I took it.

Darling! I took a step in the garden. I didn't really go out as such, but I took a step. I'm so happy. I xxxxxx

Bell, I can't wait to come back so we can walk together. Only two days left! Angus x

To Isabel.C.Ramsay@gmail.com
From Emer88@iol.ie
You won't believe this. He kissed me! Donal kissed me! As his face came closer I thought, "Oh my sweet Lord, it's going to feel like I'm being kissed by my brother," but it wasn't like that at all. It was ... right. I think we are together. Because he told me he'd wanted to get together with me for a long time, so therefore he believes we are together now.

Are we?

It's all very strange! But good!

Emer xxx

To Emer88@iol.ie
From Isabel.C.Ramsay@gmail.com
AT LONG LAST!
About time you saw what was under your nose all along!

I always rooted for Donal. You are perfect together.

I have so much to tell you too. I took my medicines! I was very, very scared they were going to poison me, but I took them! I took them for the first time two weeks ago, but I didn't want to tell you then – I wanted to make sure I could do it again, and I did.

I think I feel better. I don't know if it's just in my head or if really it's the medicines, but I feel calmer. I don't know. I always thought the medicines were the devil and maybe for some people they are very bad, but I think for me there was no other way left. They certainly didn't poison me or make me worse. It seemed so real at the time, and now the thought is ridiculous. Maybe many of my other fearful thoughts are ridiculous. Maybe I'm beginning to think normally again.

Anyway. I left the best news for last. I went outside. Just a step into the garden. But it's a beginning.

So, things are looking up. It seems incredible.

Write soon,

Yours,

Isabel x

47

No place for forgiveness

The last words I told you
Fell into silence

Isabel

The second he stepped into the house, he held me tight, tight. There was something in his embrace – a sort of need, or sense of relief – that melted me. My Angus. He was barely back, but tomorrow he would be gone again, to Glasgow. It was sad and wonderful at the same time – sad because I was going to miss him so much, wonderful because he was so much more relaxed about leaving me. He could see I was slowly, slowly climbing up.

"Show me!"

"Okay. Okay." I steadied myself and led him to the conservatory door, holding his hand. Clara stood in the background, quiet and discreet.

The grass felt soft under my feet, and Angus's arm was strong and steady.

"Come. Let's go and see the roses . . ."

But I froze. It was too soon. He stroked my cheek.

"One step at a time," he whispered, beaming.

When we walked back in, Clara was gone.

I went upstairs for a few minutes, leaving Angus downstairs to potter around. I heard the phone ringing, and after a short while Angus came back up.

"Will I make you a packed lunch for the plane?" I said with a smile as he stepped into the bedroom. I was expecting him to smile back, but the look in his eyes was bleak.

"Bell, Gillian called . . ."

I felt cold. His face told me it was not good news.

"Gillian? Is she okay?"

"Yes, she's fine. It's your dad."

And then I knew. I let myself sit on the bed heavily, as if my knees had given way all of a sudden. The world spun.

I studied my slippers. One of them had a little rip. There was an almost imperceptible stain on the carpet, right beside my left foot.

"It was quick, he . . ."

Two parallel scratches on the left slipper, the scuffed toe of the right one.

"The funeral is going to be at the end of the week, but she was hoping . . ."

I moved on to my hands. Short, white fingers, the white-gold wedding band.

"If you want to, we can just leave now. We can be in Galway by tonight . . ."

My father was dead. And we hadn't spoken for years.

He was dead.

"Bell?"

"Have you packed enough warm clothes? Clara met Inary at the shop and she said it's freezing in London right now . . ."

"Bell?"

"Yes. Have you?"

"Have you what?"

"Packed warm clothes."

Next thing I knew, Angus had taken me in his arms and I had my face buried into his neck. I was shaking with shock, my eyes dry. We stayed like that for a long time, I don't know how long, until he spoke.

"Don't worry. I won't go anywhere. I'll stay with you. Gillian was asking if we can make it to the funeral . . ." Angus tightened his hold on me, as he felt me trembling. His words resounded through me and shattered me.

The funeral.

My father's funeral.

And so it was finished. Without a word of forgiveness from either of us.

48

The way we lived

Looking back I think
I should have saved you
But I was green wood
Easy to break

Isabel

Every day was a silent day, in our house. Not before the accident, of course – but after. Before, when my mum was alive, there was warmth, and tenderness. After, there was cold – cold and silence. This was what a three-year-old had felt, without the maturity to actually *think* it, or put it into words – warm versus cold, lively versus silent, sweet versus hard. And my father was all that – cold, silent, hard.

And still, as we were growing up, Gillian and my father fitted together like two well-oiled cogs. My sister worshipped him, and he, in turn, approved of her – which was a lot more than could be said about what he felt towards me.

When I was a little girl I tried to gain his approval in every way I could – but I was always too noisy, or too daydreamy, or just *too much*. Gillian was composed, quiet, tight – I was imaginative and loud. She was a world in itself, barely opening up for my father and, later on, Maura; I was clingy, always needing reassurance, emotional in a way my father couldn't stand. I didn't understand it at the time, but as I was growing up and could decipher more and more of the situation, of my father's reasons to belittle me, I realised why it was: I was too much like my mum, and he couldn't stand it. Because he hated her, because he'd loved her too much, I don't know. Or maybe because he was afraid I would follow in my mother's footsteps.

And I did. In more than one way.

After she died, my father purged her from our home, from our lives, to the extent that I knew nothing about her. My passion for art came from within me, independently of anybody's words or influence. My father wasn't happy about me pursuing something so unlikely to earn me a living and did all he could to discourage me. I thought his hostility towards my art could not be justified by his concern over how I would support myself, that it was just too much. And then, years later, on the day of my graduation, I discovered something.

I was standing in front of my work, displayed together with that of my fellow classmates, when my sister came to me. Both she and my father had decided to attend the graduation, my father very reluctantly. I believed that Gillian had convinced him.

"Our mother loved art, you know? She had a collection of books and a few pictures she'd drawn and had framed around the house. She was very talented."

I couldn't believe my ears.

So that's where it had come from. My passion, seemingly unconnected to anything, was actually in my blood. I was so overwhelmed by emotion, my eyes filled with tears.

"Where are her pictures now?" I asked Gillian, fearing the answer.

241

"Dad gave them away. It really wasn't appropriate to keep them," she said, and her face was hard once more.

Still, I never forgot that brief exchange. I never forgot that on the day of my graduation, she had decided to share that precious memory with me.

49

Sliding

To be the one who comforts all the time
And to be the one who finally
leans his head

Angus

Bell was curled up on the sofa, her face pale and her eyes still dry. She would not cry. Which worried me even more than if she'd burst into tears.

Just what we needed: more heartache, and now, when she was making such headway in everything. I gazed at her beautiful features, her head leaning against a pillow – she was playing with her hair, as she always did when she was anxious. Suddenly I heard my phone beeping from the hall and I went fishing for it in my jacket pocket.

One more day and we can catch up, you and me. Bibi x

I'm sorry, I've had to call in and say I can't go to London. My wife's father died. I can't leave her right now.

That's terrible news. I'm so sorry.

And then,

When will I see you again? Maybe you can get away at some point, before next week?

Was she suggesting we meet up alone? All of a sudden I wanted to throw my phone away.

And still, I clutched it.

I thought of her listening to me without judging, without an agenda. Without the weight of past history, like there was between me and Torcuil.

I typed a few different replies and deleted them all. I switched the phone off and slipped it back into my pocket, and I went to take my place beside Bell.

50

Gillian

Words like walls
Between us

Isabel

With shaking hands, I called her – my sister. The first phone call I'd made in months. Even in my anguish, I couldn't help noticing that I had just overcome another fear of mine. I couldn't even remember how long my sister and I hadn't spoken. The absence of her was a thorn in my side, though I would never admit it.

Then, more than ever, I could feel how we'd never really understood each other – how we kept missing each other like two ships at night, close and yet so far, coming from the same place but going in two different directions. Two routes that would never intersect.

Her voice resounded in my ear. Her voice, so familiar to me. One I'd heard since I was born.

"It's me," I said.

"Isabel."

It squeezed my heart to hear how tired she sounded, how devastated. The loss of our father had broken her, I could feel it. They had been so close to each other.

They were not close to me.

Years of solitude rushing back to hurt me, to harden me.

"I'm sorry, I can't come to the funeral." My voice came out steelier than I wanted it to.

"Yes, well. I never thought you would."

I breathed in. That was unfair. I would have gone, if it weren't for my illness.

Would I?

Gillian snapped, "You never understood him, Isabel."

"Yes, well. He hated our mum."

"He *loved* her! When she died, it broke his heart. You always assumed she was so unhappy because of him, but you were wrong. Our mother had her own demons, and they had nothing to do with Dad."

"If he treated her like he treated me—"

"Why do you think he was so hard on you? He wanted you to be strong. To have faith in yourself. Our mother—"

"Mum."

"Mother, Mum, whatever . . ."

"When you call her Mother it sounds like you stopped loving her," I said, and I realised, embarrassingly, that I sounded like my ten-year-old self.

"Here we go again! Nobody loved her, nobody understood her but you! You didn't *know* her, Isabel. You were tiny when she died. Of course I loved her. I had ten years to love her before she left me. She left me with Dad off his head with grief, and you so small. She didn't think of us at all when she threw herself off that boat, did she? Do you remember that? Or have you forgotten that she decided to die *on a family holiday*, Isabel? You were too small, but I remember every little detail of that day!"

"You blame her!" I shouted down the phone. "You blame

her because she was sick! But you don't understand what she went through."

"Oh, and you do?"

"Yes. Because I'm sick like she was." My breath was coming out ragged with rage and pain.

A moment of silence. "Well, let me tell you this. If you do what she did, Angus is going to hate you. Hate you, Isabel." Were they tears, in her voice?

Tears for me?

"Gillian—"

"And yes, I blame her for what she did!" She interrupted me and broke the spell. "I blame her for it and I hate her more than Dad ever did. She left me. She left us. Through choice."

"Fine. Hate her if you want. Hate Mum, hate me, hate the world. See what good it does to you. Because this hate you have inside, I promise you, Gillian, it will consume you."

"Oh, really? Because, out of us two, it's me having a life. It's me having a job and children. So much for being consumed. *You're just like our mother*—"

That killed me.

I put the phone down. I couldn't listen any more. I was left shaking and full of tears, and in spite of the people who, I knew, loved me, I felt alone. So terribly alone.

Gillian was right. Not about our mum, but about me.

And I had been right too: what I'd believed through the years was not a reflection of my paranoia and insecurity – it was true.

My sister didn't care for me at all.

51

The hand that holds mine

Just go on
Just keep breathing

Angus

Once again, I was away. And my thoughts kept going home, where Bell was mourning her father and fighting her battles. Fighting hard. I wasn't talking much. I had no energy to talk. I barely had energy to play.

"Hey. How are you?" Bibi said, and her words sounded strange. Strange because usually what I heard was "How is Isabel?"

"I . . ." I needed to say I was fine. I was okay. Everything was okay.

But the weight, that night, was unbearable.

"I'm not so good," I replied, and immediately I was horrified at my admission of weakness. And the intimacy of the conversation that would follow. I wanted to turn away and go back to my rented flat; I wanted to stay and finally offload some of my worries.

"You need a drink. Come," she said, and took me by the hand. We hurried down the road under the pouring rain – an average night in Glasgow – and sat in the pub down the road. With a whisky in my hand in the warmth of the pub, I felt myself relaxing a little.

"So. I'll ask you again . . . How are you?" she said in a low voice, and slipped her hand in mine under the table. It was too much. I took my hand away gently, without making it look too abrupt.

"I'm exhausted, I suppose."

"You look it . . ."

"Thank you!" I laughed feebly.

"Are you sleeping at all?"

"Not much. I'm juggling my work and Bell and travelling up and down and being everything to everyone. That pretty much sums it up. I'd like to lie down and sleep for a week. Even just an hour without constantly worrying about my wife would be good."

"I'm sorry. You know I'm here for you."

"Thank you." I took a sip of my whisky, and the warm liquid down my throat, together with the softness of Bibi's arm rubbing against mine, went to my head. Her hair shone under a spotlight – one side of her face was in shadow, the other shone just like the moon.

"Why don't you come to my flat for a drink?" she said, without looking at me. Her eyelashes shadowed her blue eyes.

"Sure. Why not?" the whisky said for me. It sounded wrong, and I tried to stop and find some excuse, but I didn't know how. I knew I was making a mistake, but alcohol and tiredness and a sense of exhaustion – a desire, just for once, to let go – were going to my head.

The sky was white and heavy, a promise of snow. I stepped into the street, following her as she walked quickly in front of me, up two flights of stairs in a red sandstone tenement, across the threshold of her home and into a shift in my reality. And then the door closed behind us, and we were alone.

52

Roses in winter

The moment I look at the monster and see
The monster is me

Isabel

I kept fighting. Every day, a step more. Every day, a little more desire to get out of the house, a little less fear.

Clara was there, supporting me, encouraging me, calming me. "With a bit of practice, as you get better, we can go to La Piazza," Clara said with a smile. "And then Edinburgh, London, Australia, the moon!" She laughed, and I laughed with her, full of hope. *The possibilities are endless*, I thought.

Again, I was breathing the winter air, on my doorstep. The first step had been easy. And now, the second. "I'm right here, Isabel . . ." Clara kept talking, but I couldn't hear her as blood was ringing in my ears so loud, and I felt dizzy and sick, and it was so frightening . . .

One step. Two steps, once more. And then another, and another.

"We are fine. Really. It's so cold and beautiful! And maybe we can go and see the roses . . ." Clara kept whispering in my ear. "Don't be afraid . . ."

And so I kept taking steps. One, two. And another, and another. Until I reached the roses Torcuil had given me, the pink-yellow ones. There were no flowers now, of course – but there would be another spring, another summer, when I could bend over and breathe in their scent, and hear the bees buzzing around me, and feel the sun on my face. This was just the beginning.

I stood in the freezing cold with the wind on my face, and I felt joyful, so joyful – no other words could describe the simple sensation of being alive. The monster inside me awoke and did its best to force me to retreat – but I took yet another step.

"Please, Isabel. Don't make yourself regrets for when your time comes," Clara said, and her words seemed to come from long ago, from far away. "Make yourself memories," she murmured beside me.

And then it was all too much, and I felt dizzy and I wanted to get back – but I'd done it, I'd done it.

I'd gone outside.

I was not surprised when, out of the corner of my eye, I saw a blue butterfly fluttering between Clara and me.

53

Maze

I shall place
All my songs
In your hands

Angus

I blinked once, twice – a cold, white light was seeping through a gap in the curtains. Where was I? My head was sore.

All of a sudden, I remembered what happened last night with Bibi.

We'd sat together and talked, for a long time, while the rain pounded on the windows. We were both tipsy – both lonely, I suppose.

She'd leaned against me, her face close to mine, looking for a kiss.

She was beautiful, and her scent, some expensive, complicated perfume, went to my head. Her body felt warm against mine.

And then, just when I was about to fall, I'd turned my face away.

"I need to go back now, Bibi," I'd whispered.

"Why? Why can't you stay here with me?" she'd said in a voice that was like a caress. I was only human, and desire and nearly three long years of loneliness and worry and pain weighed on my heart. To just be with her. To rest and lose myself in her, for some peace, some relief. Some happiness.

But I still got up and stood in front of the door.

"I need to go," I repeated.

She looked astonished, like she couldn't believe what I'd just said.

"I thought . . ."

"Bibi, please. Please just let me go, okay? I'm sorry. I'm really, really sorry."

She was beautiful, perfect. And she understood what it was like to live for music.

But she wasn't Bell.

And so I woke up alone, and was infinitely relieved to be so. If I thought of what I'd almost done . . . If I thought of how easy it would have been to slip . . . I hated remembering Bibi's face, the dismay and disappointment as I stood up from that sofa and told her I had to go. I shouldn't even have accepted her invitation. The hard bit was that, for a moment, she'd looked very young and very hurt.

I'd asked myself why I had gone to her flat, alone.

Because I had been tempted, because I had played with fire.

Because the offer of some comfort, of sharing the burden I carried, had seemed irresistible. Yes, I had played with fire. And I'd nearly got burnt.

I wondered how she was. If she was disappointed, or sad, or if she'd deleted me from her memory already – if that day, at rehearsals, she'd pretend I didn't exist.

I grabbed my phone from the bedside table – I always kept it on, in case Bell needed me. Suddenly, just as I was looking at the screen, an email from her appeared.

From Isabel.C.Ramsay@gmail.com
To AngusRamsay@gmail.com
Good morning my love!

I have news for you.

I stood for a few minutes in our garden and oh, it was amazing. Like I'd never felt air on my face before. I went all the way to the rose bushes, can you believe it? I can't wait for you to come back and we can go for a stroll.

I love you, I love you, I love you.

Yours,

Bell

I was ashamed of my tears, but for once, they were tears of happiness.

From AngusRamsay@gmail.com
To Isabel.C.Ramsay@gmail.com
Dear Isabel,

I wrote this for you.

You are on a journey on foot. You started some time ago and you are now quite far along the road, so far that when you look back you can no longer see where you started. The path is long, but you know where you are going and you are at peace. Each day all you need to do is make that one step and you will get there. Part of this journey is to accept that until you have made many, many steps and found your path again you will sometimes experience a little pain and a little discomfort, like a stitch in your side. It's not enough to make you stop, but it reminds you that you need to pace yourself and take a breather once in a while. Sometimes the journey will take you through forests with shadows and hidden darkness and sometimes it will take you along meadows where friends will walk with you and the sun will shine and birds will sing. However, the path is the path and each step takes you closer to where you are going. It is a good place, with people you love and happiness and freedom and joy. Even though you know that the journey sometimes seems long, you know that you will be happy when you get to where you are going. Whenever you feel tired and think perhaps it's better to stop, you will see a wooden sign upon which is written the name of your destination and those thoughts will disappear. In the evening when you are resting, the deer will stand guard and watch over you while you sleep. You feel their soft breath on your face and you sleep deeply and dream of happy times.

When you arrive, you will be filled with happiness and feel proud that you kept going, and you will know that you have earned the happiness you feel. You will not be able to stop smiling. You will look back at the road you have come along and it will no longer be there.

All my love,

Angus

54

These days are mine

The moment you hold my hand anew
Because you never stopped
holding my heart

Angus

It snowed during the night, and a few snowfakes were still falling on me as I walked to rehearsals. I couldn't wait to get home; I couldn't wait to see Bell standing in our garden. When we were finished, I practically ran out of the hall, quickly saying goodbye to the conductor and to my colleagues, mumbling something about a family occasion and having to be there. That morning, practice had been endless – four hours felt like four days. On my way out, I saw Bibi out of the corner of my eye, sitting with some fellow musicians – I waved to them and they all waved back. All except Bibi, who turned away, pretending not to see me. As she turned, I caught a glimpse of her face and I saw sadness in her eyes. But it couldn't give me anything more than a small pang of guilt, as I rushed home to my Bell.

I drove probably a little bit faster than I should, the snow getting thicker and thicker as I headed north, and I was there at lunchtime. Our garden was covered in a blinding, beautiful carpet of snow, and everything was shining.

I stopped the car and, for a moment, I sat there, my heart beating fast. Hope was wrecking me, tearing me apart, because I could not bear to be disappointed. Not again, not any more.

I wanted to come in and see a smile for once. I wanted to come in and see Bell with her hands stained with paint, or busy in the kitchen, or simply lying there reading a book, relaxed, happy. The way it used to be.

I would have loved that with all my heart – because for a long time all that I had seen were tears, and all that I'd had was tension, and the shell of what my wife used to be sitting by the window, staring at the night, or cleaning obsessively, too anxious to stop. That was the way my life had been – Bell's distress rippling all around us, destroying her, destroying me.

That morning, after her joyous email, I had the feeling this time it would be different coming home. It would be coming home like it used to be.

But I was scared.

I was scared, all of a sudden, that things might have changed in the few hours it took me to arrive; that maybe that happy email was just for my benefit, that she was putting on an act for me. I had a million fears.

I stepped out of the car.

Undying

At night I don't belong
To the shores of time

Torcuil

I stopped in my tracks. There they were, Angus and Izzy –
Isabel – holding on to each other, as close as they could be. On
the doorstep of their home.

It was their moment.

I left and walked back to Ramsay Hall, joy and some other
feeling I could not name wrestling in my heart.

Snow angels

The Mystery of you
Inside my soul

Angus

A woman was standing there, wrapped in her bright-red jacket, her long, long hair loose on her shoulders. It couldn't be her, so free and brave, standing alone in the snow – but it *was*. I knew my wife's body, and I knew the way she stood, the way she moved.

And then the woman turned around and I saw her face – yes, it was Bell, her cheeks bright red in the freezing air and a smile on her face. She threw herself into the snow, arms and legs like a windmill, and stayed there.

I wanted to call Bell and wave my hands and run to her, and lie beside her in the snow, but a part of me didn't want to interrupt what seemed like a miracle. So I advanced slowly, in silence, my boots sinking at every step. The snowy driveway was like an aisle, and the trees were white and lacy, like brides.

Bell sat up and crossed her legs. She threw her head back to look at the sky and a million snowflakes fell onto her face.

"Bell!" I called, and finally ran up to her. Her face lit up when she saw me. She threw herself into my arms. We couldn't quite believe what was happening. This was us, Isabel and me, outside, laughing and hugging and kissing like old times.

"You did it on your own! I can't believe it!"

"I'm not on my own. Clara is here. Clara?" Bell turned around, left and right. "She was here a minute ago. She must have gone inside."

"I can't believe it," I said for what felt like the hundredth time. "I can't believe it."

"I can't believe it either." She looked down. "I don't know. It just happened. The snow was so beautiful. And I . . ." She shrugged. "I think I *forgot* to be afraid. I just forgot. And then I was halfway down the garden before I realised what I'd done. I'm so glad you came back, so you could see me."

After that, I couldn't speak any more. I could only kiss her mouth, her cheeks, her eyes, hold her tight, hide my face in her sweet-scented hair. She held me back, her embrace sweet and heady. She smelled of honey. And then she let me go.

"Oh, Clara, there you are!" Bell said then, and I turned around to greet Clara. She was standing just behind me, a smile on her face. I noticed she was only wearing a cardigan and her shoulders were wet from the falling snow, but she didn't seem to mind. I was about to say hello to her, but the words died on my lips. All of a sudden there was something different about her, something I couldn't quite pinpoint – a *radiance* coming from her. Her eyes shone impossibly green and her contours seemed to blur, like there was a light shining just behind her. Was it the glare from the sun? But there was no sun – it was hiding behind the grey clouds filling the sky.

"Well done, pet," she said to Bell, and I felt Bell's hand slipping into mine.

And then something incredible happened, and I realised that Torcuil was right when he'd told me he'd felt something strange, something special about Clara. Of course, he always knew. *I need to tell him,* I thought confusedly as a miracle unfolded in front of me, in front of my disbelieving eyes.

⟩

57

Isabel

Nobody will give me freedom
I have to take it
For myself

Isabel

I looked up to the sky and a million snowflakes kissed me. Finally, I had made it. I was outside, and not walking slowly, anxiously, holding Clara's hand – but unafraid, and standing on my own.

The walls of my prison had broken open, at last.

I was free.

Clara stood there. There was a strange luminosity coming off her body, like a warm, golden glow. I thought it had to be the reflection of the snow, shining white and dazzling – it took me a few seconds to realise it was *her*, that the glow was coming from within her body. And then she turned around, and all of a sudden, I recognised her.

All of a sudden a memory emerged from the depths of my soul, the memory of a beloved face, a scent, a voice – it all came back to me.

And her eyes.

Those eyes that were so similar to mine, moss green.

"Well done, pet," she said to me in her tranquil, soft voice.

I knew who she was. I knew who she was, and my lips

opened to say her name, to call her, but nothing came out, because before I could say anything, she disappeared into a soft, sweet light.

I stood, watching her dissolve, holding Angus's hand, still and silent.

"What . . . what happened?" Angus murmured when we were alone. A bird flew from a snow-covered tree, in a flurry of wings.

I told him who she was, and he held my hand tighter, his eyes wide in disbelief.

The snow was falling, falling, falling on us both.

Love Eternal

What a chrysalis believes to be the end
Is just the beginning

Clara
I shed Clara's body and my soul is bare again, translucent and naked like a sea-creature out of its shell. It breaks my heart to be away from my Isabel, but now she is free, and so am I. And now soft yet mighty ripples of wings and light surround me.

There will be no more wandering for me, no more eternal loneliness. They hold me in an embrace of light and I feel their love, and the love I feel for my daughter melts into it, and I'm full of joy.

I'm ready to finally go.

Warmth

The great silent battle
In the sprouting of a seed

Isabel

That night, Angus and I lay on the sofa wrapped in a throw, watching the flames dance in our fireplace and the snow fall outside the black window. We didn't speak much. We didn't mention Clara at all, not yet, though we knew the time would come to do that.

For now, it was all too strange, too raw for me.

I knew she wasn't coming back. I also knew she'd been there when I needed her most.

She hadn't abandoned me.

All of a sudden, an intense desire, an intense need took shape inside me.

I stood up without saying a word and wrapped myself tighter in my woollen cardigan, as the air got colder away from the flames.

"Where are you going?" Angus said lazily, trying to hold on to the folds of my cardigan. I placed a gentle kiss on his forehead and said nothing. There was a call I had to make, and I couldn't talk about it, not yet.

In the semi-darkness of the kitchen, I dialled a number, and a familiar voice answered the phone.

"Hello, Gillian? It's me."

To Isabel.C.Ramsay@gmail.com
From JSimpson@artistcom.com
Hi Isabel,

Just wanted to say, Marina from Usborne is delighted with your illustrations for Scottish Legends. *They say they're a bit dark, but very beautiful. And something else; they want* Chrysalis *too! Will write to you with all the details as soon as they're finalised. Good job, Isabel. It's great to see you doing so well and I hope I'll see you at the London Book Fair this year.*

Joanna

60

The truth about love

When all there is about you and me
Is wrapped in just a moment

Isabel, four months later

After our freezing dip, Emer and I sat wrapped in the same
blanket on the sand, shivering and drinking our scalding
coffee, made on a camping stove. We'd just been for a dip
in the freezing sea, and I felt so alive, after the cold water
had made my cheeks rosy and my blood run faster. Fatina lay
beside us, mellow as ever.

We were in Connemara, not far from Emer's house in
Galway. I'd been to visit my sister, after years of not seeing
her, and I'd finally met my nephews.

It was all like a dream, having my life back.

"You're doing so well. I'm in awe of you, Isabel," Emer said,
taking my hand with her sand-covered one. Her unfocused
blue eyes looked somewhere towards the sea, and her black
hair, wet and hard with salt, blew across her lovely face.

She was in awe of *me*? With all the challenges she faced?

"What? In awe of someone who used to be too scared to
leave the house? Are you sure?"

"Yes. Because you had one hell of a monster inside you.
And you fought it," she said, tucking a strand of hair behind

her ear. The wind danced on our faces. "You know, I often think of what is normal. To be healthy, to be sorted. To have a job and a house and stand on your own two feet. Not all of us can do that . . ." Her hand went to Fatina, stroking the dog's wet fur. "Some of us need a lot of help. Some all throughout their life, like me. The ones who manage to stand on their own are rare."

"Are you about to burst into song?" I teased her to hide my emotion. It wasn't like Emer to be so sweet; usually she made a joke of everything.

She laughed. "Call Angus for a tune. I'll sing my heart out."

Angus was still in the sea with Donal and his fiddle rested in its case in our tent. As if he'd sensed us mentioning him, he waved and called.

"Hey! Come back! It's wonderful in here!"

We laughed and shook our heads; we were too happy with our warm coffees and our blankets to get back into the cold again. I gazed at Angus's lean body and his auburn hair like a little flame in the grey of the sea. I could never express in words or even images, though it was my trade, how much I loved him. How loyal he'd been when I was ill. And I looked at Donal, and smiled, thinking of all the years he'd pined for Emer and how everything had worked out for them.

How everything had worked out for all of us.

We spent the evening chatting around the camp fire. Angus played his fiddle and Emer sang, her lovely, haunting voice rising up in the Connemara night, accompanied by the sound of the sea.

That night Angus and I crawled out of our tent, while Emer and Donal slumbered in their own, and we sat huddled up into each other. The sky was incredible, black and pure and completely limpid, dusted with a million stars.

"Oh, this is better," Angus said. "We can't possibly be inside and not look at this sky."

I snuggled even closer to Angus, my head on his chest and an arm around his waist – he was the perfect pillow.

He began listing constellations. "Orion . . . the Big Dipper . . . Cassiopeia . . ."

While he whispered, I considered how far I'd come. Only a few months before, I couldn't step over my doorstep. But after I finally managed to go outside into the garden, then I started going for walks in Glen Avich, and for coffee in La Piazza, where I finally met baby Eoin, Aisling's son. Apparently, Kate and Pablo were now working on a cruise ship, after Pablo had decided acting wasn't for him but singing was the way forward. I went shopping in Aberdeen with Margherita, at last creating and shaping a friendship with her. Finally, I went to the London Book Fair to launch *Chrysalis*. *Chrysalis* meant so much to me, because it was the story I'd started when I was still ill. There, I also met the representative of Usborne, who were thankfully not holding a grudge in spite of my previous delays in handing in the *Scottish Legends* book. In fact, they'd loved the illustrations, saying they were dark but very beautiful.

I was still taking my medicines religiously and I had started counselling to try to talk out all that happened when I was a little girl, but now I had a hold on the monster inside. In fact, I'd realised I never really had a monster inside; she was just a wee girl, the wee girl I used to be, screaming to be listened to, needing to speak out about her pain.

Finally, I'd made the momentous decision to go to talk to Gillian, my estranged sister – although there was still a lot to be explained, and a lot to be forgiven, we had at least taken a step in the right direction. We had so much to talk about, and she was as willing as me to try to understand each other, to find common ground. To mend what was broken.

And now I was in Ireland with Angus and my friends, gazing at the stars.

The mystery that had been Clara, coming to save me in my hour of need, was to remain a mystery. I could have asked myself over and over again why she disappeared, how had she come to me in the first place, what loving will had sent her to me; but there was no point. I was in desperate need and my mother had come to help. Maybe it was all I needed to know.

My mother and her green eyes, her soft hands, her silvery laugh, the way she held me when I was a baby – she'd come to me when I was desperate.

I did ask Torcuil what he knew about Clara – after all, he'd always had a "feeling" about her. He told me about seeing her in a vision at the window of my house but nothing else. I pressed him a little – but he said no more. He only said something I didn't really understand: "What you told me after the fire, let's forget about it." I had forgotten; I'd been too frightened and sore so it escaped my mind. I did ask him what it was – but he didn't reply.

Angus placed a kiss on my hair and then turned his face up to the sky again. I studied his handsome profile at the light of the glowing embers; that night his fiddle had been the sweetest sound, and once again, as always, I'd felt so proud of him. Of course, he'd gained a place in the orchestra. I knew it wouldn't always be enough for him; I knew there would be times he'd want to spread his wings even further, and travel away from me – but I felt safe in his love and I would always let him go.

I closed my eyes, letting myself drift away slowly. The best way to sleep was on my husband's chest. It was an undisputable fact.

I suppose that was the truth about love.

That night, close to Angus and wrapped up in a blanket against the breezy night, I had a dream.

My mother came to me. She stood in a field of swaying grass, a red handkerchief in her hair and her long skirt blowing in the breeze. The light of spring danced on her face. She was smiling, wrinkling up her nose, her eyes like almonds as she squinted in the sun. I was a little girl trying to stay upright in the grass that came up to my chest. I was scared for a moment, and I fell. As I lay on my back, I saw that the sky was so, so blue, and I felt her body close to mine.

She held me in her arms, and our noses touched. She was my mother.

She was Clara.

A whisper resounded in my ears, and I woke up at once, as if she'd really been whispering to me: *Don't be afraid.*

Epilogue

When I looked into your eyes
I looked into the mystery

Isabel

From the days of pain to the days of liberation, this is what I learnt: that coming on to this earth is a gift. A gift we receive through no merit of our own, the bestowing of a blessing for no other reason than love. For no other reason than life overflows, life spills out of this planet, the sky and the sea and every living creature, in an act of creation that renews itself every moment. We come into this world alone; we stand on its surface for a moment, bathed in light, and then it's all over. And every second we stand in the light, every moment is sacred; every atom of our body is sacred. From the cradle to the grave, we sing our song, brief, beautiful, unique. We are part of a force so much stronger than we can ever be – all we have to do is fall back and surrender. While the song is sung, there is no reason to be afraid, but when the song is finished, when darkness falls and fear envelopes us, that is the time to remember that still there is no reason to fear. Because when darkness comes, it's only for a moment – our atoms dissolve and renew into more life, and soon the song begins again. But until then, we live.

My mother came back to save me. She touched my eyelids with loving hands and I could see again – I could see the seasons, I could see the sky and the hills, the moon at night and the sun in the day, and a promise in the winter sky. I could see the hope of joys to come; I could see a child sitting at my table; I could see friends sitting around my fire and hands holding mine. My mother knew because she lived and she died, and what she told me when she saved me was the most simple, the most essential wisdom of all: *Don't be afraid.*

This world is full of mysteries. We believe we can decipher everything, understand everything, dominate everything. We speak and sing and scream and talk, talk, talk, so loud that the whispers of our hearts are all but lost. But when silence descends at last, that's when finally we can hear them – if we remember to listen. We trace the patterns of our lives and discover that nothing happens by chance, and nothing is just mundane, or unnecessary. That all of us were meant to be, all of us play a part in this powerful, intricate, all-encompassing web of lives and events. All of us, our lives and deaths, are miracles, and we need to make every moment hours. We need to put our regrets to rest – *and live.*